J
Buckey, Sarah Masters,-Clue ir

Napoleon Branch
Jackson District Library

W9-CHF-134

3/10/2011

Enjoy all of these American Girl Mysteries®:

THE SILENT STRANGER   A *Kaya* Mystery

LADY MARGARET'S GHOST   A *Felicity* Mystery

SECRETS IN THE HILLS   A *Josefina* Mystery

THE RUNAWAY FRIEND   A *Kirsten* Mystery

SHADOWS ON SOCIETY HILL   An *Addy* Mystery

THE CRY OF THE LOON   A *Samantha* Mystery

A BUNDLE OF TROUBLE   A *Rebecca* Mystery

MISSING GRACE   A *Kit* Mystery

CLUES IN THE SHADOWS   A *Molly* Mystery

THE SILVER GUITAR   A *Julie* Mystery

and *many more!*

— A *Samantha* MYSTERY —

CLUE IN THE
CASTLE TOWER

by Sarah Masters Buckey

Published by American Girl Publishing, Inc.
Copyright © 2011 by American Girl, LLC
All rights reserved. No part of this book may be used or
reproduced in any manner whatsoever without written
permission except in the case of brief quotations embodied
in critical articles and reviews.

Questions or comments? Call 1-800-845-0005, visit our
Web site at **americangirl.com**, or write to Customer Service,
American Girl, 8400 Fairway Place, Middleton, WI 53562-0497.

Printed in China
11 12 13 14 15 16 17 LEO 10 9 8 7 6 5 4 3 2 1

All American Girl marks, American Girl Mysteries®,
Samantha®, Samantha Parkington®, Nellie™, and Nellie O'Malley™
are trademarks of American Girl, LLC.

This book is a work of fiction. Any similarity to real persons, living
or dead, is coincidental and not intended by American Girl. References to
real events, people, or places are used fictitiously. Other names, characters,
places, and incidents are the products of imagination.

PICTURE CREDITS
The following individuals and organizations have generously
given permission to reprint illustrations contained in "Looking Back":
pp. 166–167—Kenilworth Castle, photogravure.com; woman with children,
Victorian Image Collection; pp. 168–169—London scene, Mr. P. S. Evans of
Oldukphotos.com; tourists, © Bettmann/Corbis; pp. 170–171—Statue of Liberty,
© Kit Kittle/Corbis, detail; immigrants, © Lewis Wickes Hine/Corbis;
King Edward VII, © Perry Pictures/Corbis, detail; manor house, © Steven
Vidler/Corbis; pp. 172–173—five female servants posed in front of an open
doorway, 1896–1920 (b/w photo) by Sydney Newton (1875–1960), Biddlesden
Park House, Buckinghamshire, UK/© English Heritage. NMR/The Bridgeman
Art Library; gramophone, © Dorling Kindersley, courtesy of the Museum
of the Moving Image, London; English castle, © Steven Vidler/Corbis.

Illustrations by Sergio Giovine

Cataloging-in-Publication Data
available from the Library of Congress

J
Buckey, Sarah Masters,-Clue in the castle

Napoleon Branch
Jackson District Library

For my brother, George
And my sister, Alison

TABLE OF CONTENTS

1 INVITATION FROM A KNIGHT 1

2 THE GHOST IN THE LIBRARY 20

3 MISSING TREASURE 43

4 A SURPRISE ANNOUNCEMENT 58

5 UNEXPECTED CONSEQUENCES 71

6 FOOTPRINTS IN THE SNOW 89

7 A CHASE 105

8 THE FIGURE IN WHITE 121

9 SEARCH FOR A SECRET 133

10 THE LETTER 152

   LOOKING BACK 167

1
INVITATION FROM A KNIGHT

Samantha Parkington climbed out of the horse-drawn carriage and looked around eagerly. She hoped to see London's famous British Museum. But rain was drizzling down, and the fog was so thick that Samantha felt as if she were standing in the middle of a cloud. She could hardly even see the people hurrying by in the cold January air.

"This way!" directed her grandfather, Admiral Archibald Beemis. He snapped open his big umbrella, and he and Grandmary led the way down the sidewalk, with Samantha and her adopted sister, Nellie, following close behind.

"Is it always so foggy here in the winter?" Samantha asked her grandfather.

"Not always," the Admiral replied in his crisp English accent. "Sometimes it's bright and clear. But today you can hardly see three feet ahead of you, can you? Still, I'm very happy to be here."

"I am, too," Samantha agreed. She and Nellie were both glad that their grandparents had invited them to come along on their winter trip to Europe. Samantha had been to England only once before, and Nellie had never been there. "Every proper young lady should visit England and France," Grandmary had told the girls when they left New York. "You'll learn more in a few weeks of travel than you could ever guess."

"It will be a great adventure, too," the Admiral had added with a smile.

Their voyage across the Atlantic Ocean *had* been an exciting adventure. Ever since their ship had docked five days ago, the girls had been busy seeing the sights of London, the world's biggest city. Samantha loved hearing English accents wherever they went, and she loved English customs such as sipping tea in midafternoon, spending pounds and pence instead of dollars and cents, and, best of all, riding on the top of a double-decker omnibus.

Together, she and Nellie and their grandparents had visited Buckingham Palace, where tall soldiers in red jackets solemnly stood guard in front of the gates. They had listened to the chiming of Big Ben, the great bell in the Clock Tower of Westminster Palace. They had even watched tigers and lions pacing in their cages at the London Zoo.

But almost every day, smoky-smelling fog had lingered over the city. Today the fog was so thick that it was almost choking. Grandmary held her handkerchief over her face as they walked up the steps to the British Museum, and Samantha could hear Nellie, who had been sick in the past, coughing.

There were muffled sounds from people passing close by, too. Through the fog, Samantha heard a man call, "Henry, Ian! Are you out here?" Then, in a lower voice, he added, "Where can those young rascals be?"

It would be easy to get lost today, thought Samantha, peering through the gloom. Then the Admiral opened the door to the British Museum. As she stepped inside, Samantha blinked at the lights in the entrance hall. Crowds of well-dressed people were strolling through the hall. It was as if a hidden city had suddenly come to life.

"In this museum, you'll see treasures from all over the world," said the Admiral proudly. He folded his umbrella and tucked it under his arm. Then he paid sixpence for a museum guidebook. "The only question is, where should we go first?"

While the Admiral and Grandmary studied the guide, Samantha craned her neck to look up at the marble statues around the entryway. Suddenly she heard a clatter behind her.

"I beg your pardon!" a man exclaimed.

Samantha turned and saw a white-haired man reaching down for the Admiral's umbrella, which now lay on the floor. "I should have watched where I was going," the man apologized. Then he stopped and looked closely at the Admiral. "Dash it all, Archie, is that you?"

"Charles!" declared the Admiral. "Why, it's been ages! How are you, old boy?" The two men slapped each other on the back and shook hands enthusiastically. Then the Admiral introduced Grandmary, Samantha, and Nellie to his good friend and former schoolmate, Sir Charles Stallsworth.

Sir Charles! thought Samantha, amazed. *Could he be a British knight?* She had read about knights in castles, but she had never imagined that she'd meet a real knight in modern London.

"This is a pleasure, indeed!" said Sir Charles. The knight was short and stout, and he wore a wool coat instead of a suit of armor. His white hair and thick white eyebrows stood out against his ruddy complexion, and he beamed as he shook hands with Grandmary. "Archie, you're a lucky man to have such a lovely wife—and granddaughters, too!" he added with a bow toward Samantha and Nellie.

"My own dear wife, Emily, passed away six months ago. I miss her every day," Sir Charles told the Admiral and Grandmary. He shook his head sadly. "Emily and I were never blessed with children of our own. My twin nephews are orphans, though, and they are living with me now."

Samantha and Nellie looked at each other. Both girls were also orphans. Samantha's parents had died in an accident when she was very young. Nellie's immigrant parents had died of the flu, leaving Nellie, who had worked as a maid, alone to care for her little sisters, Bridget and Jenny. Not long ago, Samantha's Uncle Gard and Aunt Cornelia had adopted all the girls, and now Samantha felt lucky to be part of a big, happy family. *It must have been hard for Sir Charles's nephews to lose their parents **and** their aunt,* Samantha thought sympathetically.

"I brought the boys to the museum today," Sir Charles continued. He sounded annoyed. "Their tutor and I were just looking for them."

"Are they lost?" asked Grandmary. There was concern in her voice, and Samantha looked around the crowded entrance hall. She did not see any lost-looking little children.

"I'm sure they're quite fine," said Sir Charles. "We have a train to catch, though, and they were supposed to be here half an hour ago."

Sir Charles lowered his voice. "My nephews are a fair bit of trouble," he told Grandmary and the Admiral confidentially. "They were suspended from their boarding school a few weeks ago. Apparently, they spent all their time making up foolish inventions instead of doing their lessons—and they stole pies from the kitchen, too. The headmaster says he's not sure if he wants them ever to come back."

Those boys do sound like a lot of trouble! thought Samantha.

"Perhaps there was a misunderstanding," said Grandmary hopefully.

"Perhaps," Sir Charles agreed with a sigh. "I'd better go back to British Antiquities, where I saw the boys last. They may have forgotten that we were to meet here at the front entrance."

"We'll go with you," offered the Admiral. "It will give us a good starting place for our visit."

"Splendid!" declared Sir Charles. He led the way through the museum, marching quickly through rooms filled with ancient treasures. As Samantha and Nellie passed through the Egyptian Gallery, they stole quick looks at the mummies in coffins. Samantha shivered to think that the mummies had been dead for thousands of years.

Next, they came to long galleries filled with Greek and Roman art. Stone sculptures lined both sides of the galleries. Nellie looked at the statues and then glanced quickly away. "I guess people didn't wear many clothes back then!"

"Jeepers!" exclaimed Samantha. "I guess not!" Both girls giggled.

They climbed a wide set of stairs to the second floor. The museum was quieter up here. Their footsteps echoed as they passed through rooms filled with ancient art. When they arrived in the room marked "British Antiquities," they were the only visitors in the gallery.

"Well, it seems the boys aren't here either," said Sir Charles with a frown. Then he brightened. "But since we're here, come look at this."

Sir Charles strode over to a display case, and the others followed him. "See that bronze plate there?" he said, pointing to a greenish piece of metal at the back of the case. "It was armor for a horse going into battle. I found it outside my castle and donated it to the museum."

Do knights still have castles? Samantha wondered as she leaned to get a closer look at the armor. She had read about castles in fairy tales, but it was hard to believe that people actually lived in them.

"Emily left me a small legacy in her will, and I'm using it to restore Lockston Castle," Sir Charles explained to Grandmary. "It's been in my family for generations. It was once a favorite visiting spot for kings, too!" Sir Charles gestured to the armor on display. "Someday, I hope to open the whole castle to the public, so visitors can learn its history."

"Does your castle look like the ones in pictures?" Samantha asked the knight.

Grandmary gave Samantha a stern look, as if to remind her that children should not interrupt when their elders were talking. But Sir Charles chuckled. "It's not *quite* like the castles in books—at least not yet," he said. "It needs extensive repairs. We live next door, in the manor house."

"I recall visiting you at the manor house when we were boys," said the Admiral, smiling. "Remember the night we spent looking for Sir Reginald? I don't think I was ever so scared in my life! Your father was furious when he heard about it."

Samantha looked up at her grandfather. It was hard to imagine that the Admiral had ever been scared of anything. *Who is Sir Reginald?* she wondered.

Sir Charles clapped a hand on the Admiral's shoulder. "I say, Archie, why don't you and your family come stay with me at Lockston? You could come down by train tomorrow."

"That's very kind of you, but..." the Admiral began.

"It's not kind at all—I'd love a bit of company!" Sir Charles insisted. "I'm tired of rattling around the house by myself. And you could get out of this foggy city for a few days and show your granddaughters the English countryside." He smiled at Samantha and Nellie. "Wouldn't you like to visit the castle, girls?"

"That'd be wonderful!" Samantha blurted out. She could already imagine herself exploring a castle.

"Oh, yes!" added Nellie, her eyes bright with excitement.

The Admiral and Grandmary shared a glance, and Samantha saw her grandmother nod. "Thank you, Charles," said the Admiral. "A visit to the countryside would be just the thing. We couldn't stay more than a day or so, though. We're leaving for Paris on Thursday."

"Even a short visit would be splendid!" exclaimed Sir Charles. "My nephews will be delighted, too—if I can find the rascals."

Just then, a pair of boys with masses of freckles and unruly brown hair burst into the room. They were followed by a thin, balding man with a cane. "Ah, there you are at last," Sir Charles greeted them. He introduced his nephews, Ian and Henry, and their tutor, Mr. Fisher. Samantha was surprised to see that the twins looked about twelve years old— the same age she and Nellie were. From the way Sir Charles had talked about the boys, she had expected them to be much younger.

Grandmary shook hands with the twins. Then she smiled and asked, "How shall I tell you apart?"

"*I'm* the good-looking one!" Ian and Henry said at the same time, and then they both exploded in laughter. It was obviously one of their favorite jokes.

Grandmary's eyes widened with surprise.

"Remember your manners, boys," Sir Charles said sharply. He frowned at the twins. "Where have you two been? Did you forget our meeting time?"

The twins stifled their laughter. They both were short and plump, and they were wearing identical gray suits with stand-up collars. The only difference Samantha could see between them was that Henry had slightly more freckles on his pink cheeks and Ian seemed a bit shyer. They reminded Samantha of her friends Agatha and Agnes, twins who were always thinking up mischief.

"We had a very good idea..." Henry began. He grinned at Samantha and Nellie, as if he hoped that they would enjoy the joke.

"It didn't work out exactly as planned, though," Ian added, and then he grinned, too.

"What's this about, Mr. Fisher?" asked Sir Charles.

"Ian and Henry were trying to sell some, er, items they'd found in Lockston Castle," said Mr. Fisher. He leaned on his cane as he spoke, but his voice was surprisingly strong. "A guard thought perhaps the boys had taken the items from the museum, but I was able to clear up the misunderstanding."

Sir Charles turned to the boys. "What on earth were you trying to sell?"

"These arrowheads, Uncle," said Henry. He pulled two small triangle-shaped items from his pocket and held them in his palm for everyone to see. Samantha looked closely. The triangles were made of metal, and they had hollow stems where arrows had once been attached.

"Aren't they beauties?" asked Henry. "We thought if people came to the museum to see old stuff, surely they'd want to buy arrowheads from the castle."

"Yes, and besides, we need money to buy new parts for our bicycles," Ian chimed in.

Sir Charles's ruddy complexion turned even redder. "The Stallsworths don't sell family treasures!" he scolded the twins. "And you boys are not allowed to steal away artifacts from the castle grounds, either."

"We didn't *steal* the arrowheads, Uncle," Henry protested. "We *found* them."

Before Sir Charles could reply, Mr. Fisher coughed politely. "Excuse me, sir, we don't want to miss the last train to Lockston."

Sir Charles took a deep breath. "Quite right,"

he agreed. He turned to the Admiral and Grandmary. "Let me show you the train schedule. The trip takes only two hours, and I'll have a carriage meet you at the railway station."

While the grown-ups talked, Henry and Ian began to toss one of the arrowheads back and forth between them. "Are you coming to the castle?" Henry asked the girls.

"Yes," Samantha replied. "Your uncle just invited us."

"Oh," said Ian as he caught the arrowhead. "I'm glad you're not scared. Most girls probably would be."

Nellie frowned. "What's there to be scared about?"

Henry turned to look at her. "The castle's ghost, of course!" he said, and the arrowhead fell with a clink to the floor.

The next afternoon, the shrill sound of a train whistle split the air as the train from London

arrived in Lockston Village. A carriage with
two horses was waiting at the railway station.
The driver, a small man with a large mustache,
tipped his cap to the Admiral and then loaded
their trunks onto the carriage. Samantha, Nellie,
Grandmary, and the Admiral all climbed inside
the carriage, and Grandmary's maid, Doris, sat
in front with the driver.

The air was crisp, and there were puffs of
white clouds in the sky as they drove through
the village. Samantha looked out the window
eagerly as they passed by thatch-roofed cottages,
small shops, and an old stone church. When
they reached the outskirts of the village, they
followed a road with a rapidly flowing river
on one side and snow-covered pastures on the
other side. They drove past a broken bridge,
where men were working, and several farmhouses, where flocks of fat geese waddled in
the yards.

After about a mile, the carriage turned onto
a winding drive lined by trees on both sides.
Branches of the trees formed an archway over

the narrow road. Beyond the trees stretched wide fields dusted with snow. "Oh, this is pretty!" whispered Nellie.

As the carriage turned a corner, Samantha saw, far ahead, a vast three-story stone building with massive gray columns. "What's that?" she asked curiously.

The Admiral smiled. "That's Lockston Manor, where we'll be staying."

"Gracious sakes!" blurted Nellie.

"Jiminy!" exclaimed Samantha. "It's so big."

"It *is* quite a large home," Grandmary agreed. "But remember, Samantha, it's not polite to point. And I hope you and Nellie will be on your very *best* behavior during our visit. The English landed gentry live a bit more formally than we do in America."

"What are landed gentry?" Nellie asked.

"They are families, like Sir Charles's, who have owned lands in England for generations— and have helped to rule the country," Grandmary explained. Then she hesitated. "They are proud of their family history, and they have some customs that are different from ours," she added. "In a house like Lockston, for example, children often spend their days with their tutor or governess. So you and Samantha may stay in a different part of the house than the Admiral and I, and you may eat your meals separately, too." Grandmary smiled. "I'm sure you girls will be fine, though."

Samantha decided to ask a question that had been bothering her. "Is it true that there's a ghost at Lockston Castle?" she asked her grandparents.

"Of course not!" said Grandmary quickly.

But the Admiral looked out the window for a moment before answering. "Well," he said at last, "Sir Charles's ancestor, Sir Reginald, was a famous knight. Sir Reginald died just outside the castle, and there's a legend that his ghost can be seen on moonlit nights. Charles and I once spent all night searching for the ghost, though, and we never saw it."

They were getting closer to the manor house now, and Samantha saw that a steep hill overlooked the house. At the very top of the hill, two rugged stone towers rose into the sky. The towers looked dark and ominous against the white clouds.

That must be the castle! she realized, and a chill ran up her spine.

2

THE GHOST IN THE LIBRARY

Snow crunched under their wheels as the carriage rolled up the circular drive to Lockston Manor. Two carved stone lions guarded the tall front door of the manor house. As soon as the carriage pulled to a stop, a young footman opened the door and ushered Grandmary, the Admiral, Nellie, and Samantha into a high-ceilinged entry hall with dark wood paneling and a long, curving staircase.

Ancient-looking portraits hung on the walls of the entry hall, and an empty suit of armor stood in a shadowy corner. For a moment, Samantha felt as if she'd stepped into another museum. Then Ian and Henry came racing down the staircase. "They're here! They're here!" the boys shouted.

The footman gathered their coats and hats, and Sir Charles came out to welcome them. He asked if they would like to have tea first or see the manor house, and Grandmary and the Admiral asked to see the house.

"Splendid!" declared Sir Charles. Starting off at his usual brisk pace, he led them to an enormous dining room. It had floor-to-ceiling windows and a mahogany table that looked as if it could seat twenty guests. Gold-framed portraits hung in this room, too, and Sir Charles pointed out pictures of Stallsworths who had been generals in the army, advisors to kings, and important members of Parliament.

As they examined the portraits, Samantha noticed that the white and gold wallpaper in the room was faded and in one corner it had peeled away from the wall.

"We have some repairs to do in here," said Sir Charles with a wave of his hand toward the peeling wallpaper. "But come, look at my study. I'm working on a book about the history of Lockston Castle. Mr. Fisher is helping me with the research, and my goddaughter, Lady Florence, has been taking photographs of the castle."

"She's been looking for the ghost, too," murmured Henry, who was standing at the back of the group.

Is there really a ghost? wondered Samantha as Sir Charles showed them into the next room. It was bigger than any study she'd ever seen. Its windows looked out onto the snowy fields, and a fire crackled in the marble fireplace. Instead of a desk, there was a heavy-looking mahogany table, where a typewriter and a wind-up gramophone sat beside piles of books. Above the table hung a large corkboard with photographs of the castle pinned on it.

"Florence is the daughter of my cousin, the Earl of Norwood, and she's a clever girl—she takes quite good pictures," said Sir Charles, gesturing toward the photographs. "Her parents wanted her to go to Egypt with them for the winter—they hoped she might meet an eligible young British Army officer there. But Florence refused to go. She insists that she wants to find a job with a newspaper instead of getting married, of all the foolish things!"

"Times are changing so fast," said Grandmary sympathetically. "Some girls from the best families want to get jobs these days, just as if they were men."

"Of course, Florence's father disapproves of her silly ideas about a career," said Sir Charles as he continued to the next room. "He's permitted her to help with the book this winter, but as soon as her parents return from Egypt in the spring, she's going straight home again." He looked around absentmindedly. "I wonder where she is now."

"Probably campaigning for women's right to vote!" said Henry in a low voice. Ian snickered.

Samantha and Nellie both glared at the boys. Aunt Cornelia campaigned for votes for women, and the girls would never allow anyone to make fun of their beloved adoptive mother.

Sir Charles next showed them the drawing room—a large room with blue satin chairs and somewhat faded blue curtains—and then the adjoining ballroom, a wide, nearly empty room with a tall ceiling painted light blue and trimmed with gold.

"I especially want to show you the library, Archie," said Sir Charles as he set off down the hall again. "I remember you used to like rare books, and Emily's collection was her pride and joy. Some of the books are real treasures—they're among the most valuable things in the house."

"I'd very much like to see them," said the Admiral eagerly.

But as soon as Sir Charles opened the library door, a voice called out, "Stop! Wait!" There was a flash of bright light inside the room. Then the voice said reluctantly, "All right, you may come in now."

As Samantha stepped into the library, she saw a pretty young woman with fiery red hair emerge from under the dark hood of a camera. The young photographer looked businesslike in a high-necked white blouse and floor-length black skirt, but Samantha guessed that she was only eighteen or nineteen years old. Sir Charles introduced her as his goddaughter, Lady Florence Frothingham.

"I didn't know you planned to take photographs in here today, Florence," said Sir Charles after they all shook hands. He sounded puzzled.

"There's so much history in this room, Uncle," said Lady Florence. She stepped back behind her camera, as if impatient to be snapping pictures again. "And isn't this the room where the housemaid saw Sir Reginald's ghost?"

"Well, so she claimed, but she was a silly woman. She was probably imagining things," said Sir Charles offhandedly.

Still, Samantha felt uneasy. *Sir Reginald's ghost was seen **here**?* she thought. She looked around the room. It was lined with oak bookshelves and had the musty smell of old paper. A full-size portrait of a silver-haired woman hung over the fireplace, and in the center of the room stood an antique desk surrounded by several chairs covered in red velvet. The red curtains that covered the floor-to-ceiling windows were open slightly, and Samantha could see the hill where Lockston Castle stood. She was struck by how close the ruins seemed.

Grandmary smiled at Lady Florence. "We don't want to get in the way of your photography. Perhaps we should come back later."

"Yes," agreed Sir Charles, stepping back into the hall. "We'll come back later." He turned to Grandmary and the Admiral. "Why don't we go back to the drawing room. We shall have tea, and then Mrs. Grissom, my housekeeper, will take you to your rooms."

Henry spoke up. "Could we show the girls the castle now, Uncle?"

"They'll surely want to see it," added Ian.

"I've no doubt you boys want another excuse to get away from your schoolwork," said Sir Charles, frowning. Then he shrugged. "You may go, but be back soon. You must not be late for your tea."

Grins spread across the boys' faces. "Come on!" said Henry. The four children retrieved their hats, coats, and gloves from the elderly butler, Mr. MacDougal. Then the twins led the way outside. As they hurried up the rocky path toward the castle, a cold wind was blowing. Samantha pulled her hat down over her ears and thrust her hands into her coat pockets.

"You don't think we'll see the ghost, do you?" Nellie asked Samantha quietly.

Samantha glanced upward. The sun was setting, and it shed a rosy glow on the gray stone castle. "I don't think ghosts come out while it's light," she said, trying to sound confident. "And we should be back before dark."

"Let's hurry!" said Nellie, walking faster.

When they arrived at the top of the hill, Samantha stopped short and stared at the castle ruins. "Goodness gracious!" she whispered.

Ahead, two tall stone towers stood on either side of an archway that was so massive, it looked as if a giant had built it. Thick walls connected the towers and encircled the ancient castle. The stone walls were still standing. But looking through the archway, Samantha could see that the castle was in ruins.

"We found the arrowheads right here," said Ian proudly, pointing to the ground underneath the archway.

"They might've even belonged to one of Sir Reginald's archers," Henry added.

Sir Reginald again! thought Samantha. "Why was Sir Reginald so famous?" she asked the boys.

"He was a hero," said Ian. He tossed a fist-sized stone high into the air. It banged on another stone and then rattled down the hill. "He fought at Agincourt!"

"What's that?" asked Nellie.

"You don't know about the Battle of Agincourt?" demanded Henry.

Nellie shook her head. "Never heard of it," said Samantha.

Ian rolled his eyes. "It's only the most famous battle ever fought!" he declared. "The English were outnumbered, but they beat the French on Saint Crispin's Day in 1415. Sir Reginald was one of the knights who won the battle."

"Sir Reginald helped lead the soldiers," said Henry proudly. "But he was wounded in the battle, and his servant and horse were killed. He was coming home from France by himself when a band of thieves attacked him in the night, just outside the castle walls."

Samantha looked down the steep hill. She tried to imagine the tired, wounded soldier struggling to get home, only to be met by more fighting. *It must have been terrible*, she thought.

"Sir Reginald was stabbed, and he died before his family even knew he was here," Henry concluded. His voice dropped to a whisper. "It's said that's why Sir Reginald's ghost walks at night. People say they've seen him carrying a light—as if he's still searching for his family."

A cold gust of wind blew through the ruins. Nellie tightened her shoulders. "We should go back to the manor," she urged.

Ian tossed another stone. "We can't go back so soon! Our tutor will make us do lessons before tea."

"We promised we wouldn't stay long," Samantha reminded him.

"Wait!" exclaimed Henry. He pointed down the hill. "What's that?"

As soon as Samantha turned to see where Henry was pointing, she felt her hat slip off. She spun back and saw Henry running through the archway, waving the hat above his head like a prize.

"If you want it, you'll have to catch us," he shouted. Then he and Ian disappeared inside the castle.

"That's my new hat!" Samantha cried, sprinting after them.

"We'll get it back," said Nellie with a look of determination.

The girls went through the archway and looked around at the ruins inside. Among the piles of stone, Samantha saw a massive fireplace and a half-ruined wall that rose into the sky and then stopped in midair. The boys were nowhere in sight.

Samantha heard scuffling noises and laughter behind her. "They're hiding in one of the towers!" she said.

Samantha and Nellie ran to the open doorway of the nearest stone tower. Inside, they
found a narrow circular staircase that rose up
into the shadows. The only windows were slits
set high in the wall, and they let in hardly any
light. Cautiously, Nellie started up the stairs,
with Samantha close behind. Some of the steps
were almost knee-high, while others were
crumbling. Samantha nearly slipped when she
put her foot down and discovered that half a
step was gone.

"Be careful," she whispered to Nellie. "Some
of the steps are broken."

"I know," Nellie whispered back. "I almost
fell."

The girls kept climbing until they reached
the lookout at the top of the tower. The small
perch, enclosed by a waist-high wall, was
empty. The wind was even colder up here, but
Samantha could see for miles. Below her lay
the manor house, the road they had taken from
the village, and the river that ran alongside the
road. In the distance, the sun was sinking lower

in the sky, and there were purplish streaks along the horizon.

Samantha turned and looked out over the castle ruins. The shadows on the walls were growing longer, but there was no sign of movement. Samantha fought back a shiver. "I don't see Ian or Henry anywhere," she told Nellie.

"Maybe they're in the other tower," Nellie suggested, and she started down the stairs. As Samantha followed her, she caught a glimpse of something dark on the stone floor of the lookout perch. She reached for it, hoping that it might be an arrowhead. But when she picked it up, she saw that it was only a button that had become wedged on its side between the stones. She thrust the button into her pocket before hurrying down the winding stairs.

The second tower was almost identical to the first, and it was empty, too. But when the girls reached the lookout perch, they could see Ian and Henry. The boys had somehow doubled back and climbed into the first castle tower. They were sitting on top of the parapet, dangling their feet and twirling the hat. "You can't catch us!" they teased from across the archway.

Suddenly, a deep voice boomed, "Ian! Henry! Get down from there this instant." It was the tutor, Mr. Fisher, and he was limping up the hill quickly.

Samantha and Nellie giggled as they watched the boys scramble off the parapet. The twins reached the castle entrance soon after Samantha and Nellie did, and a moment later Mr. Fisher limped through the archway.

"You boys have been gone much too long," said Mr. Fisher. "What have you been doing up here?"

"Oh, nothing," said Ian, kicking up the snow with his foot. "We just wanted to show the girls a bit of the castle."

"Samantha's hat blew away and we had to get it back for her," added Henry. "Here you are," he said, bowing slightly as he handed Samantha the hat.

The tutor looked at Samantha questioningly.

She brushed off the hat. It wasn't harmed, and she decided that she did not want to get the twins into trouble—even if they deserved it. "We *did* get to see a lot of the castle," she said, planting the hat firmly on her head.

"The boys were telling us that the castle is haunted. Is that true?" Nellie asked the tutor.

"I've heard the legend," said Mr. Fisher. He glared at Ian and Henry. "But I think that even more mischief goes on here than we know about." With his cane, he motioned toward the archway. "We'd better get back before dark."

When they returned to the manor, the young footman opened the door before they even had a chance to knock. "Hello, Roger!" the boys said as they tossed their coats to him.

A tall, thin woman wearing a white cap stepped into the entry hall. "I see you're back at last," she said with a frown. "I'll have your tea sent up to the schoolroom."

"Thank you, Mrs. Grissom," said the tutor. He handed his coat to the footman. "I must get some books from the library for my research," he told the twins as he headed down the hall, his cane clicking on the polished floor. "Go upstairs now, and get cleaned up before tea."

Ian was already halfway up the stairs. He stopped and leaned over the railing. "Roger, will you tell Cook to send up lots of bread and jam with the tea?" he called to the footman. "We haven't eaten in hours!"

"Samantha and Nellie are hungry, too," added Henry. "They particularly said they'd like plenty of scones." Then he raced upstairs after his brother.

"We said no such thing!" Nellie protested to Roger.

"We didn't mention scones at all," Samantha added.

Roger was smiling as he headed for the kitchen, but Mrs. Grissom's frown deepened. "Please come with me, girls," she said. "I'll show you to your room."

The housekeeper started up the staircase, a big ring of keys jangling at her side. She stopped at a windowed seating area at the top of the stairs, where hallways led off to the right and the left.

"This is the south wing," said Mrs. Grissom, gesturing to the carpeted hallway on the right. Lamps glowed all along this hall, and the walls were hung with portraits in gilded frames. "The Admiral and Mrs. Beemis will be staying there," she added with a tight smile.

Then she turned to the left, and her smile evaporated. "You girls are in the north wing, in the room that used to be the schoolroom."

As the housekeeper led them down the long hallway on the left, Samantha noticed that there were fewer portraits here, the polished wood floor was bare, and only one of the brass lamps along the walls was lit. They passed one closed door after another. Samantha asked, "Are lots of other people staying in this wing, too?"

"No," said Mrs. Grissom. She sounded

surprised by the question. "You girls will be the only ones."

Mrs. Grissom opened a door at the very end of the hall. Samantha and Nellie stepped into a bedroom with a pair of windows that looked directly out at the castle. *This room must be right above the library,* Samantha realized, and her heart sank.

She glanced around the room. It was furnished with two brass beds, a nightstand, two dressers, and a tall wardrobe. But there were no decorations, and the big room felt cold and strangely empty. Across from the beds, there was a fireplace with a mirror above it. A girl in a white apron and cap was arranging a fire, and she looked up, startled, as they entered.

The girl was small and thin, and when she brushed her curly light brown hair back from her face, she left a streak of dust across her cheek. Mrs. Grissom scowled at her. "Finish up quickly, Mabel. Cook will need help in the kitchen."

"Yes, ma'am," said the young housemaid.

Mrs. Grissom turned to Samantha and Nellie.

"You'll be having your meals in the schoolroom on the second floor. Tea will be served soon. Please go up as soon as you are ready." She nodded toward the maid. "You may let Mabel know if there is anything else you need."

"Thank you," said Samantha. She was about to ask a question, but Mrs. Grissom had already turned to leave. Her keys jangled as she hurried down the hall.

"Why did Mrs. Grissom tell us to go up to the second floor?" Samantha asked Nellie. "Aren't we on the second floor already?"

"I think they say it differently here," said Nellie, whose parents had come from Ireland. "My mum and dad used to call the first floor the 'ground floor,' and what we'd call the second floor, they'd call the first."

"Oh!" said Samantha. "I guess *lots* of things are different here." She turned to Mabel, who was lighting a match. "Do you know where the schoolroom is?"

"Yes, miss," said Mabel, and her gray-green eyes met Samantha's for the first time.

She's not any older than Nellie and I are, Samantha realized.

"The schoolroom *is* on the second floor, near the servants' rooms," Mabel continued. "The stairs are across the hall. I clean up there every day."

"Have you worked here long?" Samantha asked her.

"No, miss," said Mabel. She touched the match to the kindling, and an orange flame flared up. "I began last summer. Before that, I went to school in my village, across the river from here. I was first in my class, too," she added with more than a hint of pride. "Best in spelling *and* in arithmetic." She paused. "But when I turned twelve, I left school."

That must have been hard, thought Samantha. "Do you miss school?" she asked.

Mabel gazed at the floor. "I'm glad to have a job, miss, and to be able to help my family."

"Samantha! We'd better unpack," Nellie called to her across the room. There was a warning tone in Nellie's voice.

Samantha went to the nearest dresser and looked in the drawers. All her clothes were folded, and her travel journal and pencils were neatly arranged. Grandmary's maid, Doris, had even put pine-scented sachets in the drawers. Samantha's silver brush and comb were set out on top of the dresser, too.

"I think Doris has already done everything," she told Nellie.

The fire was burning brightly now, and it illuminated the room. Mabel was busy arranging the fire screen, but Samantha could see the maid's pale face in the mirror. Samantha decided to ask her about Sir Reginald. "We heard there's a ghost who haunts the castle on moonlit nights. Have you ever seen it?"

In the mirror, Samantha saw Mabel's gray-green eyes widen in fear. But a moment later, the look was gone. "No, miss," Mabel said in a hollow voice. Then she turned around and, keeping her eyes on the ground, she asked, "Is there anything else, miss?"

"No, thank you, Mabel," Nellie said gently.

Mabel curtsied and hurried from the room.

As soon as the door shut behind the maid, Samantha turned to Nellie. "It seemed as if Mabel was scared—and she could hardly wait to get out of here. Do you think she knows something about the ghost?"

Nellie's forehead creased in a frown. "Maybe. But more likely, she was scared that she'd get into trouble for talking to us. The ladies that I worked for *never* let me talk to anyone."

Samantha nodded thoughtfully. She and Nellie had first become friends when Nellie had worked as a maid for Mrs. Ryland, Grandmary's next-door neighbor in Mount Bedford. Mrs. Ryland hadn't approved of her servants talking to friends, so the girls had had to meet in secret in the backyard.

"Poor Mabel!" said Samantha, sitting down on one of the beds. "I wonder if it's lonely for her in this big house. Out here in the country, she wouldn't even have a neighbor in the next yard to talk to—and she doesn't go to school anymore, either." Samantha stared for a moment at the brightly burning fire. "I surely didn't mean to get her into trouble."

"Don't worry. Mrs. Grissom wasn't here, so she won't know," Nellie assured her. "And I'm sure Mabel *is* lonely—I know I would have been if I'd had to work in a house like this." Nellie shuddered at the thought. "I wish there was some way we could help her."

"I do, too," said Samantha. With a pang, she remembered how frightened Mabel had looked.

Was it really the housekeeper she was afraid of? Samantha wondered. *Or was it the ghost?*

3
MISSING TREASURE

When Samantha and Nellie stepped out of their room a few moments later, they heard a crash on the floor above. "What was that?" asked Nellie, stopping dead.

Samantha listened. There was a loud bump. Was someone hurt? "We'd better go look," she said, her heart thumping.

Across the hall, a door opened to a wooden staircase that rose steeply to the floor above. As Samantha cautiously opened another door at the top of the stairs, a blur flew by her. She opened the door wider and stared. It was Henry, and he was riding a bicycle. At the far end of the hall, he skidded to a stop in front of what looked like a pile of pillows stacked up against the wall.

Ian raced up to the girls on another bicycle.

"Hello!" he said, smiling. "Is it time for tea?"

"Your uncle lets you ride bicycles inside the house?" asked Samantha, astonished. She looked down the servants' hall. It was wide and uncluttered, with no pictures or decorations on the walls, and the floor looked as if it hadn't been polished in a long time.

"Oh, yes," said Ian matter-of-factly. He put his feet on the ground. "We're inventors, and we need to test out our bicycles. Besides, we're the only ones up here—except for the servants, of course. So we don't bother Uncle at all."

"He said that if we promised never to ride on the stairs, we could ride up here whenever we liked," added Henry. "Do you want to try? We've been working on the brakes, and I think we've finally got them just right."

Samantha and Nellie looked at each other. Then they both nodded. Nellie borrowed Ian's bicycle, and Samantha borrowed Henry's.

"This is fun!" Samantha cried delightedly as she and Nellie pedaled across the smooth floor of the servants' hall.

As they neared the far wall, she heard one of the boys yell, "Steer into the pillows if you can't stop."

Nellie screeched to a halt a few feet from the wall. Samantha tried to brake, too, but the bicycle kept rolling. Nellie dodged to one side just as Samantha crashed into the pile of pillows. As she tumbled from the bicycle, a blizzard of feathers flew up around her.

"Samantha, are you all right?" asked Nellie anxiously.

"The bicycle's not hurt, is it?" called Henry.

"I'm fine," said Samantha as she dug herself out from the pillows and picked up the bicycle. "And so's the bicycle. But the brakes don't work at all! Why didn't—" Samantha stopped midsentence as she saw the housekeeper, Mrs. Grissom, appear in the hallway.

Oh no! thought Samantha. She and Nellie exchanged a glance, and then they quietly walked the bicycles back down the hall.

Mrs. Grissom stood with her arms crossed over her chest. "You must stop playing these silly games!" she told the twins. "Someone could get hurt—and look what a mess you've made." The housekeeper shot a glance toward Samantha.

Samantha looked down and saw feathers clinging to her skirt. Behind her, a trail of white feathers littered the hall.

"They're not silly games!" Ian objected. "We're inventors, and we're working on a new kind of brakes—we just don't have them quite right yet."

"Inventors indeed," sniffed Mrs. Grissom. "Of all the nonsense!"

Footsteps sounded from the stairway, and Mr. Fisher limped into the hall with a book under his arm. He was followed by a stocky young woman with blond hair who was carrying a silver tray.

"The twins have been up to mischief again," the housekeeper told Mr. Fisher.

"Boys will be boys, Mrs. Grissom," said the tutor calmly. He turned to the maid. "You may take the tray into the schoolroom, Daisy."

"Come on, let's eat," said Henry. He and Ian started toward the schoolroom door.

Mr. Fisher held out a restraining hand. "Ladies first," he reminded them.

Samantha and Nellie filed into the schoolroom, followed by Ian and Henry. Half of the large room was crammed with toolboxes and bicycles in various states of repair. The other half held a blackboard, a long table surrounded by chairs, and piles of books. Across from the table, tall windows looked out at the rocky hill and the castle ruins.

While Mr. Fisher and Mrs. Grissom talked in the hall, the children took seats at the table. Samantha glared at the twins. "You got us into trouble!"

"You said you were allowed to ride bicycles up here!" added Nellie.

Henry snatched a cucumber sandwich from a platter. "No," he said between bites of the sandwich. "I said *Uncle* doesn't mind if we ride our bicycles. I didn't say anything about Gruesome Grissom."

"Gruesome hates us," said Ian. He picked up a small china pitcher. "But at least Cook likes us—she sent up plenty of cream for our tea today." Samantha watched in surprise as Ian poured a generous helping of thick cream into his cup and then handed the pitcher to his brother, who did the same. *Maybe it's an English custom*, thought Samantha, who preferred lemon in her tea.

She could hear Mrs. Grissom's shrill voice in the hallway. "Really, Mr. Fisher, I know it's not my place to complain to Sir Charles. But I have a hard enough time running this house with such a small staff, and housemaids won't stay because of all the talk about that ghost. I can't have the children making more work for everyone."

Samantha sucked in her breath. *Housemaids won't even stay here because of the ghost!* she thought. *And now Nellie and I are in the north wing by ourselves.*

Mr. Fisher limped into the room and calmly took a seat at the head of the table. "Now, boys, remember your manners. Henry, please offer the cream to the young ladies."

"No, thank you!" declared Samantha.

"None for me, either," said Nellie hastily.

Mr. Fisher smiled. "I'm afraid the boys started adding cream to their tea when they were at Bristwell." He stirred his tea. "I prefer milk, myself."

Samantha thought about the conversation she had just overheard. "Have many people seen Sir Reginald's ghost?" she asked Mr. Fisher.

But Henry answered first. "Just last week, a maid swore she saw the ghost in the library. She quit the next day."

"Have *you* ever seen the ghost?" Nellie asked the boys.

"Not yet," Ian admitted. "But we were living at Bristwell before, so we were here only on short visits."

"Now that we're living here, we're going to find him!" promised Henry.

CLUE IN THE CASTLE TOWER

Later that evening, Samantha and Nellie had supper in the schoolroom. Then, soon after they returned to their own room, there was a knock at the door. Samantha opened it cautiously. It was the twins.

"We're going to look for the ghost tonight. Do you want to come—or are you too scared?" Ian challenged them.

"We're not scared!" Samantha replied, even before she had time to think.

"That's right!" Nellie agreed bravely.

"Let's start in the library," Henry said with a grin. "Come on!"

Samantha and Nellie followed the boys down the winding staircase. As they neared the ground floor, they could hear laughter coming from the dining room on the other side of the main hall. "What's that?" asked Nellie.

"Your grandparents and Uncle are still at dinner," whispered Henry. "We'd better be quiet if we don't want them to hear us."

"I'll bet they're having lots of food," said Ian wistfully. "Uncle always does."

"Don't you eat in the dining room, too, sometimes?" asked Samantha.

"We used to on holidays, when Aunt Emily was alive. She was jolly, and she always ordered cakes for us," said Henry. They reached the bottom step and turned right, toward the library. "Now we eat in the schoolroom, and Uncle eats by himself."

"Oh," said Samantha. She remembered the lively dinners she and Nellie had at home with Uncle Gard, Aunt Cornelia, Bridget, and Jenny. They all liked to sit together and talk about their days. She felt a twinge of sympathy for Ian and Henry. *I guess they really do live differently than we do*, she thought.

As the children tiptoed away from the entry hall, the sound of laughter grew fainter. When they came to the closed library door, Henry whispered, "I'll make sure it's safe." Then he slipped inside.

Samantha and Nellie shared an uneasy glance as they waited for Henry to return. After a few moments, the door opened again. Henry beckoned to them, and Samantha, Nellie, and Ian shuffled into the room single file. Silently, they stood clustered around the antique desk in the center of the library. Outside, the moon was shining on the snow. Slivers of light came through the gaps in the heavy library curtains. It was just enough for Samantha to see the vague outlines of Nellie and the twins standing next to her.

I'm sure we're the only ones here, Samantha told herself as she tried to peer into the dark corners of the library. *There's nothing to be scared of.*

Then a muffled wail broke the silence. Samantha gasped. It sounded like no other sound she'd ever heard. She felt her heart hammering in her chest. The wailing noise was coming from the windows. *Could the ghost be right outside?*

"Gracious sakes!" Nellie whispered. She grasped Samantha's arm.

The muffled noise rose and fell, like someone crying out for help.

"We should see what it is," said Samantha, trying hard to sound braver than she felt.

"Don't, Samantha," Nellie warned in a trembling voice. "Maybe the ghost's out there..."

Samantha heard a snorting noise in the darkness. Then someone turned on the small desk lamp. "Ha, ha!" Henry crowed.

"We borrowed Uncle's gramophone!" Ian exclaimed. He yanked open the curtains. On the floor, a record on the gramophone was going round and round. Samantha could now hear the wailing clearly. It was the sound of the record playing.

"We tricked you!" cried Henry. He doubled over in laughter.

Nellie's face was white. "It wasn't funny."

"It was dumb!" declared Samantha. "And I think—"

But before she could tell the boys what she thought, the door opened. Grandmary came into the room, followed by the Admiral and Sir Charles, who switched on the overhead light.

Sir Charles looked startled to see the children. "Why are you in here?" he asked the boys sternly.

"We were showing our guests the new gramophone," said Henry, his cheeks turning bright red.

"It's very interesting," added Ian as he rushed to pick up the machine.

"Indeed?" said Sir Charles sternly. He raised his white eyebrows. "Take the gramophone back to my office immediately, and then go upstairs. I'll discuss this with you in the morning."

As Henry and Ian hurried out of the room with the gramophone, Sir Charles turned to Samantha and Nellie. "I was about to show the library to your grandparents," he said in a kinder tone. "You girls may each choose a book to read, if you'd like. The most valuable ones are in the locked cabinet, but you may borrow any book you find on the open shelves. My wife had quite a large selection."

Samantha looked around the library and saw hundreds of books to choose from. "Thank you!" she said. Nellie nodded, too.

"Lady Stallsworth must have loved books," said Grandmary gently.

"Oh, yes," Sir Charles agreed. "I'm afraid I've never been much of a reader myself, but these books were Emily's treasures. That's why I hung her portrait in here." He looked up at the painting that hung over the fireplace and smiled wistfully. "It's as if she is still with me whenever I'm in this room."

Samantha studied the portrait. It showed a distinguished-looking woman with blue eyes that matched her bright-blue dress. She looked kind, and there was a hint of a smile on her face. As Samantha looked up at the painting, she could easily imagine that Lady Stallsworth herself might walk into the library at any moment.

No wonder Sir Charles misses her so much, thought Samantha. *And Henry and Ian, too.*

Samantha turned away from the portrait and began to look for a book to read. On a shelf at the back of the library, she was excited to find a collection of Sherlock Holmes stories that she had never read before. She was leafing through its pages when she overheard Sir Charles describing the rare books in the nearby glass cabinet. "Emily was especially fond of her first edition of *Paradise Lost*," said Sir Charles proudly. "It's belonged to her family for generations."

"Such a book is indeed a treasure!" the Admiral declared. "Any collector would be thrilled to have one of the first editions."

Samantha heard the clink of keys as Sir Charles unlocked the door of the cabinet. Curious to see what this special book looked like, she tucked *The Return of Sherlock Holmes* under her arm and joined her grandparents. "What are first editions?" she asked her grandfather.

"They are the copies that came off the printing press the very first time the book was printed," the Admiral explained. "Often books are changed slightly in later printings, so first editions become quite valuable, especially for famous works such as *Paradise Lost* or Shakespeare's plays."

"Oh!" said Samantha, peering at the fragile-looking volume that Sir Charles held out to the Admiral. Her grandfather put on his glasses and opened the book with utmost care.

Samantha watched as her grandfather slowly turned the pages. She was surprised to see him frown after a few moments and then hold the book to the light.

Finally, the Admiral looked up. "I'm afraid there's been some mistake, Charles," he said quietly. He closed the book. "This isn't a first edition. John Milton published *Paradise Lost* in 1667. This was printed much later."

"That's impossible!" Sir Charles exclaimed. He snatched the volume from the Admiral and examined it himself. Then he looked up with a stunned expression. "A thief must have stolen the original!"

4
A SURPRISE ANNOUNCEMENT

As the words *thief* and *stolen* echoed through the quiet library, Samantha looked at the glass case. Nothing in it seemed to have been disturbed. The books were all neatly ordered. How could a thief have broken into the manor house and stolen the precious book without anyone noticing?

Grandmary spoke up. "Perhaps the first edition has been misplaced," she suggested. "It might even be hidden behind another book. Shall we see if we can find it?"

Sir Charles ran his hand through his white hair. He looked shaken. "Yes, I suppose that would be a good idea," he agreed.

"Let's get started right away," said the Admiral. Then he turned to Samantha and

Nellie. "You girls have had a long day. You'd best go to bed."

"Could we stay and help look for the book?" Samantha offered.

"No, my dears," said Grandmary firmly. "We will see you in the morning."

As the girls climbed the staircase to their room, Samantha realized that she still had the Sherlock Holmes book in her hand. *I guess it's all right to take the book upstairs,* she told herself. *I'll be sure to return it before we leave.*

Upstairs, there was only a single light on at the top of the stairs. Shadows seemed to follow the girls as they walked down the long hall of the north wing. Samantha tried hard not to imagine that anyone could be lurking in the darkness. When she and Nellie reached the safety of their room, Samantha switched on the small lamp between their beds.

"That's better!" said Nellie with a sigh of relief. The girls got ready for bed as quickly as they could. A maid had set out their flannel nightgowns and put a hot-water bottle in each bed. But Samantha's teeth chattered even after she got under the covers. She wasn't sure if it was because she was cold—or because she was still scared.

Nellie must have felt just as worried. "Samantha," she whispered from her bed, "you don't think the *ghost* could've stolen the book, do you? A maid saw the ghost right there in the library."

Samantha shivered harder. "I—I've never heard of a ghost stealing anything," she said. She tucked her blankets tightly around her and warmed her feet on the hot-water bottle. "I'll bet it was the boys. Maybe they're playing a trick on Sir Charles. They're as bad as Eddie Ryland was!"

Eddie Ryland had lived next door to Samantha in Mount Bedford, and he had often teased her and played mean tricks. After his mother hired Nellie as a maid, Eddie had tried to make life miserable for both girls.

"Eddie was terrible!" Nellie recalled. She thought for a moment. "I don't think Henry and

Ian are mean," she said. "They just like to play tricks. I wish we could get back at them for that trick tonight. I was scared half to death."

"Me too," said Samantha with a shudder.

For a long time she lay in bed, unable to fall asleep. She was staring at the orange embers in the fireplace when she heard the creak of floorboards. It sounded as if someone was walking down the hall.

Samantha bolted up in bed, her heart pounding. Mrs. Grissom had said that no one else was staying in the rooms along this hall. *Who could be out there?* she wondered. *Could it be the thief? Or even the ghost?*

"Nellie, are you awake?" Samantha whispered. There was no answer from the other bed.

Samantha listened hard. She could hear the clicking of shoes on the hardwood floor. And then she heard the creaky sound of bicycle wheels turning.

"It's those boys again!" thought Samantha. Her fear suddenly turned to anger. "I'll bet they're trying to play another trick on us!" She jumped out of bed, determined to stop whatever trick the twins were planning.

But when she swung open the door, no one was there. Samantha glanced down the hall. At the far end, a petite woman in a black coat was hurrying toward the stairs. It looked like Lady Florence, and she was pulling a very small two-wheeled cart.

Why is Lady Florence up so late? Samantha wondered as she got back into bed. *And where is she taking that cart?*

Samantha felt wide-awake now, and she tossed and turned, thinking about the strange events of the night. Finally, she decided to get her book from the dresser. As she was passing the tall window, she saw a flash of light out of the corner of her eye. Samantha stopped still. What could have made that flash? It seemed much too cold for thunder and lightning.

She stared out at the castle. The tall towers were silhouetted against the sky in the moonlight. As she watched the ruins, she found herself shivering again. She remembered that the ghost had been seen carrying a light.

It couldn't have been the ghost, she told herself. *It just couldn't have been.*

A light flashed again. It was so quick that Samantha would have missed it if she had blinked. Suddenly, she remembered the flash of light she had seen in the library that morning. It had come from Lady Florence's camera.

Lady Florence must have gone out to take photographs at the castle, Samantha thought. She felt her fear fade away. *That would explain everything!*

She climbed into bed, turned the light off, and pulled the covers over her head. She felt warm at last. But before she drifted off to sleep, she wondered, *Why would Lady Florence try to take pictures in the middle of the night?*

When Samantha opened her eyes in the morning, Mabel was standing in the room, holding a tray with two china cups and saucers. "Here's hot chocolate for you," Mabel said.

Smiling shyly, she put the cups on the bedside table. "Mrs. Grissom said to tell you that morning prayers will be held in half an hour."

Samantha was still groggy. "Morning prayers?" she repeated.

"Yes, miss," said Mabel. "There are always prayers before breakfast." She opened the curtains and sunlight streamed in.

"We'd better hurry!" said Nellie, swinging her feet onto the floor.

"Yes, miss," Mabel agreed. She picked up the empty tray. "Will there be anything else, miss?"

"No, thank you," said Samantha. "And you don't have to call us 'miss.' I'm Samantha and this is Nellie."

Mabel stared down at the ground. "Yes, Miss Samantha," she said, and quickly carried the tray out of the room. Samantha bit her lip. She had only wanted to be friendly, but it seemed as if everything she said just made things worse.

As the girls washed their faces and dressed, Samantha told Nellie about the footsteps she had heard the night before—and the lights she had seen at the castle. "When I looked out the window, I thought it might be the ghost," Samantha said. Nellie's eyebrows shot up, and Samantha hurried to reassure her. "But the flashes must've been from Lady Florence's camera," she continued.

"Oh," said Nellie, relaxing. After a moment, she added, "I didn't know you could take pictures at night."

"I didn't, either," admitted Samantha. "But what else could it have been?"

As soon as they were dressed, Samantha and Nellie stepped out of their room. This morning, light was shining brightly through the large windows at the end of the hall, and there was a faint smell of bacon cooking somewhere in a distant kitchen. "I guess we should go up to the schoolroom for prayers," said Samantha. "Mrs. Grissom said we'd be eating our meals up there."

Samantha and Nellie discovered that the table in the schoolroom was set for breakfast, but no one was in the room. "Maybe we should look downstairs," suggested Nellie.

The girls were just about to leave when Samantha noticed a pitcher of cream on the table, right next to the sugar, salt, and pepper. She picked up the pitcher. "Nellie," she said slowly, "do you remember when Eddie Ryland put salt in the ice cream at my birthday party? It tasted terrible."

Nellie's eyes widened. She understood Samantha's idea immediately. "Oh, Samantha! Do you think we should?"

"Why not?" Samantha said boldly. "Ian and Henry keep playing tricks on us—and it would teach them a lesson."

Nellie grinned. "It would be fun."

Samantha quickly heaped salt into the cream pitcher, and Nellie stirred it up. Then, giggling, both girls headed out into the hall. They almost collided with the blond housemaid, Daisy.

"Oh, Miss Samantha and Miss Nellie!" said Daisy, flustered. "You'd best hurry or you'll be late for prayers. Everyone else is already in the main hall."

A SURPRISE ANNOUNCEMENT

Daisy sounded so worried that Samantha and Nellie half ran down the winding staircase to the entry hall. There they found Sir Charles, the twins, Mr. Fisher, Grandmary, and the Admiral all standing together on one side of the hall, while the servants were gathered on the other side. Samantha and Nellie squeezed in next to Grandmary, just a few feet away from Ian and Henry.

The boys looked serious in their ties, dark gray jackets, and starched white shirts. But they whispered to each other when they saw Samantha and Nellie. Samantha wondered what new tricks the twins had in mind for today. *They'll be surprised!* she thought, smiling to herself. She glanced at Nellie, and both girls nearly broke into giggles again.

Trying hard not to laugh out loud, Samantha turned away from Nellie and looked around the hall. She was surprised by how many servants were assembled in the hall. Mrs. Grissom, who looked as sour-faced as she had the previous day, stood in the front. Daisy and Roger were standing at the outer edge of the servants' circle, and the elderly butler, Mr. MacDougal, was standing behind them. In the back was a plump older woman whom Samantha guessed was the cook. Finally, in the corner, there was Mabel, who stood off by herself, staring at the ground.

She does look lonely, thought Samantha, and once again she wished they could be friends.

As the clock chimed the hour, Lady Florence rushed into the hall. "Sorry!" she said as she wedged herself behind Samantha and Nellie. Sir Charles cleared his throat and began to read from the Bible.

After prayers were over, he snapped the Bible shut and looked around at the assembled group. "I regret to have to tell you this," he said, his thick white brows knit together. "But last night I discovered that more than a dozen rare and valuable books are missing from the library. I believe they have been stolen."

More than a dozen books! thought Samantha, shocked. She had thought that only one book was missing. *If this is a trick, it's a very mean one,* she decided. She glanced over at Henry and Ian to see what their reaction might be. There was no hint of mischief in the boys' faces, only surprise.

"The most important missing book is a first edition of *Paradise Lost*, by the poet John Milton. It's not only very valuable, but it was treasured by Lady Stallsworth, and so it means a great deal to me, too," Sir Charles continued.

He paused for a moment. The only noise in the hall was Henry, shuffling his feet. "I am offering a reward of one hundred pounds for the book's safe return—or for information that leads to whoever took it," Sir Charles announced. His eyes slowly scanned the faces around him. "The reward will be payable immediately."

A murmur of surprise spread through the room. Daisy whispered, "One hundred pounds! It'd take me years to earn that much."

Samantha swallowed hard. She'd known that the volume was important to Sir Charles. But she had never guessed that it could be worth so much money. She glanced again at Ian and Henry. Both boys were staring at their uncle with their mouths open. They seemed truly shocked by the news.

Maybe they didn't take the books, thought Samantha. *But if it wasn't the twins, who was it?*

5

UNEXPECTED CONSEQUENCES

After morning prayers, Samantha felt a gentle hand on her shoulder. It was Grandmary. "It seems I've hardly seen you and Nellie since we arrived," she said quietly. "Did you girls sleep well last night?"

Samantha remembered how frightened she had been by the footsteps in the hall. But after that, she had slept soundly till morning. "Yes, Grandmary, we did sleep well."

"I'm glad," said Grandmary. "Your grandfather and I will be going out with Sir Charles later. We've been invited to visit some old friends in a nearby village. I'll be sure to stop by your room before we leave."

Samantha watched the Admiral escort Grandmary into the dining room for breakfast.

They both looked serious—as if the news of the theft was weighing heavily on their minds.

With a sigh, Samantha followed Nellie, the twins, and Mr. Fisher up to the schoolroom. As she climbed the stairs, Samantha kept thinking about the stolen books. She remembered how neatly everything had been arranged in the glass cabinet. It hadn't looked at all as if a robber had broken in and ransacked the library. And why had Sir Charles told the entire household that there would be a reward for the safe return of the book? It was almost as if he thought that someone in the house might be hiding information about the theft.

Could the thief be living here right now? Samantha wondered. *Could it be someone who was standing with us at prayers this morning?*

When she stepped into the schoolroom, Samantha saw that the servants had filled the table with platters of eggs, bacon, smoked fish, and buttered bread. There were pots of tea and hot chocolate on the table, too, and suddenly Samantha remembered the cream.

UNEXPECTED CONSEQUENCES

Oh no! she thought. She had been so worried about the missing books, she had forgotten all about the trick she and Nellie had arranged for the boys. *Maybe the joke isn't such a good idea*, she decided. *Not on a day like this, when everyone is upset about the stolen books.*

She saw Henry pick up the cream pitcher. "May I have the cream, please?" she asked him hastily. She hoped that she could pour all the cream into her own cup before anyone else tasted it.

But it was too late. Henry had already helped himself and then passed the pitcher to his brother. Ian filled his cup to the rim before passing the pitcher on to Samantha. With a sinking heart, she realized that the pitcher was now almost empty. The boys' tea would taste terrible!

The boys were wolfing down bacon and eggs when Sir Charles came into the schoolroom. He sat down at the only empty place at the table.

"Would you care for some tea, sir?" asked Mr. Fisher, offering him a cup. Both Samantha and Nellie froze for a moment.

Sir Charles waved the cup away. "No, no," he said. "I've come to talk to my nephews." He turned to the boys. "Did you understand what I was saying downstairs?"

"Yes," said Henry between bites of food. "*Paradise Lost* is lost!"

Ian grinned, and then he lifted his teacup and took a drink. A strange expression came over his face, and he made choked, gasping noises into his napkin.

"Are you *laughing,* young man?" Sir Charles barked at him. "This is a serious matter!" He looked sternly from one twin to the other. "I know you boys are fond of pranks, but those books are very valuable to me. If you've had anything to do with their disappearance—anything at all—I want you to tell me right now."

Henry and Ian looked down at their plates, but Ian still held his napkin over his mouth.

"I'm quite sure that neither of the boys would take anything from the library, sir," Mr. Fisher said quietly. He turned to Henry. "Would you?"

UNEXPECTED CONSEQUENCES

Henry had just taken his first gulp of tea. He managed to gasp, "No, sir," before he covered his face with his napkin. He hunched over, his shoulders heaving. Samantha and Nellie exchanged a guilty glance.

Sir Charles pulled himself to his feet. His face was red with anger. "I've been patient with you boys for too long," he thundered. "First, you disgraced yourselves at Bristwell, then you tried to sell the castle's arrowheads—and now you have the impudence to laugh when I ask you serious questions. Well, I'll have no more of your foolery! I don't care what it takes—I'm sending you back to Bristwell next week!"

Ian dropped his napkin. His face was white. "But, sir—" he began.

"Silence!" ordered his uncle. Then he turned to the tutor. "Mr. Fisher, a word with you, please."

Mr. Fisher followed Sir Charles out of the room. Left alone at the table, Henry made a face, and then he wiped his mouth. "What was in that tea? It tasted disgusting."

"Absolutely awful!" agreed Ian. "I thought I was going to, well, you know—right at the table!"

Samantha pushed back her chair. "I'm sorry. It was my fault," she confessed. Then she told the boys about the salt that she had poured into their cream.

"I helped," Nellie added. "And I'm sorry, too."

"We thought it would be a good joke, after all those tricks you played on us," Samantha explained. "We didn't realize it would turn out like this." She stood up. "I'll go tell Sir Charles what happened. Then he'll know that you weren't laughing at him."

Henry held out his hand to stop her. "No, don't!" he warned.

"Why not?" asked Samantha.

"If you say anything now, it'll only make things worse," Henry explained. He nodded at the pitcher. "And we don't blame you for the joke. You girls were good sports not to tell on us before. We'd never tell on you now."

"Besides, if Old Fish can't talk Uncle out

of sending us back to Bristwell, nothing you could say would make a difference," Ian added glumly.

Samantha sank back down and stared at her bacon and eggs. "What kind of school is Bristwell, anyway?" she asked the twins.

"It's a boarding school for 'young gentlemen'—boys from wealthy families and all that," said Henry. "But the lessons are boring, and the headmaster is a bully. It's a horrible place."

"Bristwell is worse than horrible!" Ian declared. "And the other boys there hate us."

"Why?" asked Nellie.

"We don't have lots of money, and we're not good at games," Henry said with a shrug. "We're short, too."

Ian nodded. "We might as well wear a sign that says 'Kick me.'"

Nellie, who had once lived in an awful orphanage, said quietly, "I understand."

"Did you tell your uncle how bad Bristwell is?" asked Samantha.

"We tried to," said Ian. "He won't listen at

all. He says we must be exaggerating and we shouldn't tell tales."

"We stole from the kitchen at Bristwell because we *wanted* to be sent home," Henry continued. "We hoped Uncle would let us stay here till we're old enough to go to college. We want to become engineers and make bicycles that can climb mountains—and go really fast, too!" For a moment, Henry's eyes shone with excitement. Then he shook his head. "But Uncle says our inventions are a waste of time."

"Now that Uncle thinks we took his old books, he'll probably never even let us come home for holidays," said Ian gloomily. He looked around the schoolroom. "And we won't get to work on our bicycles, either."

"Maybe Sir Charles will find out who really took the books," Samantha suggested. "Then he won't be angry at you anymore."

Both boys were silent. Nellie looked at them questioningly. "Are you sure you don't know *anything* about the books that were stolen?"

"Very sure," said Ian, meeting her gaze.

"We'd never have taken Aunt Emily's books—ever."

"Of course not," Henry agreed. "And if we knew who had taken them, we'd tell Uncle. But it could have been almost anyone."

"The bookcase was locked," Samantha reminded him. "Whoever the thief was, he—or she, I guess—must've had to get the key."

"Lots of times, Uncle Charles leaves his ring of keys in the study," said Henry. "I saw them yesterday, when we borrowed the gramophone. Anyone could've taken them—and then put them back."

"*Paradise Lost* may have been lost for a long time, too," added Ian. "Ever since Aunt Emily died, Uncle Charles hardly ever looks at the rare books. He might never even have known the books were missing if he hadn't wanted to show them to your grandparents."

"What if—" Samantha began.

Just then, Mr. Fisher returned to the room. All four children looked up at him hopefully. But Mr. Fisher shook his head. "I'm sorry, boys," he said to Ian and Henry. "I'm afraid you'll have to go back to Bristwell. And I—well, I suppose I'll have to look for another job."

Mr. Fisher took up his fork, and the rest of breakfast was eaten in silence.

After the meal was over, the girls returned to their own room. A housemaid had tidied while they were gone. The two brass beds were neatly made up, the carpets looked freshly swept, and a fire was burning brightly in the grate.

"Why did I *ever* copy Eddie Ryland?" Samantha exclaimed as soon as she shut the door. She flopped down on her bed. "Henry and Ian will have to go back to Bristwell—and it's all my fault!"

Nellie sat down on her bed. "I thought that trick was a good idea, too, remember? Besides, if the boys weren't always playing jokes on other people, we never would have played a joke on them. And Sir Charles might not have gotten so angry at them, either."

"I guess you're right," said Samantha. "But I still feel terrible." For several minutes, she stared out the window. "Nellie," she said finally, "maybe *we* can find out who stole the books. Then the twins won't have to go to Bristwell."

Nellie looked doubtful. "We're only going to be here until tomorrow. And we wouldn't even know where to start. It sounds as if almost anyone could've taken the rare books."

"Only someone in the house would've known where the keys were kept," Samantha persisted. "So chances are, the thief is someone who lives here. Maybe we can find out who it is."

"But it's a huge house—and there are lots of people here," Nellie pointed out.

"We could start by making a list of everyone we know," Samantha offered. She went over to her dresser and rummaged in the top drawer. Then she pulled out a pencil and a piece of paper and began to search for a book to write on.

"That's funny," Samantha said, looking at the

nightstand. "I put my book right here last night. Now it's gone."

"It's over there, on the mantel," said Nellie. She glanced toward the fireplace.

"I know I didn't leave it there," murmured Samantha. She picked up the book and thumbed through it. "Were you reading it?"

"No," Nellie said without concern. "I'm reading *Heidi*, remember?"

Samantha frowned. When she'd last stopped reading, she had been near the end of the book. Now the ribbon marker was at the beginning. *That's odd*, she thought.

With a shrug, she sat back down next to Nellie and, resting her paper on the book, wrote:

> *Mr. Fisher, tutor*
> *Lady Florence, photographer*
> *Mrs. Grissom, housekeeper*
> *Mr. MacDougal, butler*
> *Roger, footman*
> *Daisy, maid*
> *Cook*

Samantha paused, her pencil poised above the paper. "What about Mabel?" she asked Nellie. "She's our age and she hasn't worked here very long. I don't think she could be the thief."

"It doesn't seem likely," Nellie agreed. She thought for a moment. "But I guess it's only fair to include everyone."

Reluctantly, Samantha added:

Mabel

Both girls studied the list for a moment. "Everyone seems nice," Nellie said at last. "Except maybe Mrs. Grue—Grissom. It's hard to imagine *any* of them stealing from Sir Charles." She looked up at Samantha. "Maybe the books were just misplaced somewhere."

"But Sir Charles *did* look for *Paradise Lost* last night. And so did Grandmary and the Admiral. They couldn't find it."

"We could look again," Nellie urged. "It would be terrible if Ian and Henry got sent back to Bristwell just because someone put a few books in the wrong place."

"You're right," Samantha agreed. She folded up the list of suspects and put it in her drawer, tucking it underneath her long underwear so that no one would find it. Then she and Nellie started down the hall. The enormous house was eerily silent, and they walked quickly. But before they reached the staircase, a familiar voice called, "Samantha! Nellie!"

Samantha looked up and saw her grand-mother coming toward them from the south wing. Grandmary had changed clothes since breakfast, and now she was wearing an elegant pale gray dress trimmed with satin. A matching hat, long white gloves, and a beautiful string of pearls completed her outfit.

Grandmary looks like a queen, Samantha thought proudly.

"Where are you girls off to in such a rush?" asked Grandmary as they met at the top of the staircase. "I was just coming to say good-bye to you before we leave."

"We're going to the library," said Nellie.

Samantha glanced out the window and saw

Lockston Castle on the hill. She knew that, since they were leaving tomorrow, this might be the only day that she and Nellie could explore the castle. "We'd like to go outside, too," Samantha told her grandmother. "May we walk up to the castle while you are gone?"

"Yes, I suppose so," said Grandmary with a smile. "It certainly looks like a nice day outside. Be sure to bundle up, though. And if you go into the library, be careful to put all the books back exactly where you find them. I don't want to worry Sir Charles further. He is quite upset by the theft of his books."

"Do you think a thief really stole the books, Grandmary?" Samantha asked. "Nellie and I had an idea—maybe someone just put the books back in the wrong place."

"Or borrowed them and forgot to return them," added Nellie.

Grandmary shook her head regretfully. "No, my dears, I'm afraid not. You see, someone not only *stole* the rare books but also *replaced* them with newer versions of the same books.

The newer books look similar, but they aren't valuable at all."

Samantha was puzzled. "How could that have happened?"

Grandmary took a deep breath. "Whoever stole the books must be educated enough to know which rare books are most valuable— and clever enough to plan the theft quite carefully."

It can't have been an accident after all, Samantha realized. Then another thought occurred to her. "Why is Sir Charles sending Ian and Henry back to their school? He can't believe the boys would have done all that."

"Sir Charles cares very much about his nephews, and I am sure he is doing what he feels is best for their future," said Grandmary quietly. "But the boys have been in trouble many times. It's possible their uncle believes they would be better off at boarding school than here at home."

"But that's not fair," Samantha protested. "The boys didn't take the books—I'm sure of it.

There must be something we can do to help them."

"We are guests here, Samantha," Grandmary cautioned her. "We should be careful not to interfere unless our help is needed."

*But Ian and Henry **do** need our help,* Samantha thought. Before she could say anything, Doris came bustling down the hall. "I have all your things ready for the trip, madam," she said in her loud voice.

"Thank you, Doris," Grandmary replied. Then she turned back to the girls. "Your grand-father's friends live on the other side of the river. Because the local bridge is out, it will take us a while to get there, and we may be back quite late tonight. If you need anything while we're gone, talk to Doris or the tutor, Mr. Fisher."

Samantha and Nellie nodded. "Yes, Grandmary."

Grandmary hugged them both. "Be good, my dear girls, and I'll see you tomorrow."

Samantha gave her grandmother an extra-long hug and breathed in the lilac scent that

Grandmary always wore. Then Grandmary went back to the south wing while Samantha and Nellie hurried down the winding staircase.

"Grandmary and the Admiral would *never* send us to a school we hated—and neither would Uncle Gard or Aunt Cornelia," Samantha whispered to Nellie.

"I feel sorry for Henry and Ian," said Nellie thoughtfully. Nellie had a faraway look in her eyes, and Samantha wondered whether she was remembering the orphanage where she and her little sisters had once lived.

"It must be hard for the boys now that Lady Stallsworth is gone," Nellie continued. "They have all this"— she gestured toward the wide entry hall—"but Sir Charles doesn't seem to want them around."

Nellie turned, and her face was suddenly serious. "You're right, Samantha. We have to find out who stole the books."

6
FOOTPRINTS IN THE SNOW

The door to the library was open a crack, and Samantha peeked in. She didn't see anyone inside. There was only Lady Stallsworth's portrait over the mantel, looking down at the girls.

"Come on!" Samantha whispered. She and Nellie slipped into the dimly lit library and shut the door behind them. They headed straight for the cabinet where the rare books were kept under lock and key. Samantha squinted through the glass at the dark, leather-bound books neatly lined up on the shelves. "I'm not surprised Sir Charles didn't notice that the books had been changed," she said. "I can't even see the titles."

Nellie stepped over to the window. "Here," she said, drawing aside the heavy curtains. "Is that better?"

"Much better," Samantha said. Light now shone into the library. Samantha could clearly see the polished bookcases and the beautiful antique desk. She realized what a cozy room it was. *No wonder Lady Stallsworth liked to spend time here,* she thought.

"Samantha, come here!" Nellie called.

"Did you find something?" asked Samantha as she hurried over.

Nellie nodded and pointed to the ground on the other side of the tall windows. Samantha leaned over and looked out. In the bright sunshine, she could see the faint outline of footprints on the snow-dusted ground. Directly under the window, a small patch of snow had been trampled.

"It looks as if someone climbed through this window!" Samantha exclaimed. She turned to Nellie. "Let's see where the footprints came from!"

Leaving the manor house was more difficult than Samantha had expected. First, she and Nellie had to find the footman, Roger, and ask him where he had put their coats and hats. Roger insisted on fetching the coats himself, but he allowed the girls to follow along as he opened the door to a small, almost hidden coatroom near the main entrance, where all the outdoor clothes were kept.

Mrs. Grissom walked by while Nellie and Samantha were buttoning their coats. The girls had to stop and explain where they were going and when they'd be back. "And you are quite sure your grandmother approved this?" the housekeeper asked suspiciously.

"Oh, yes," Samantha assured her.

"Very well," said Mrs. Grissom. "Please remember that your luncheon will be served in the schoolroom in an hour."

"We'll be back," Nellie promised.

By the time the girls stepped outside, a brisk breeze was blowing. Snowflakes skittered across the frozen ground and glistened in the wind.

Samantha pulled her hat tightly over her head as she and Nellie walked around the house to the library window. When they reached the window, they looked around to be sure that no one was watching them. Then they stooped down to examine the prints.

There were three or four tracks in the patchy snow, but the wind was already blurring their outlines. All Samantha could see was the suggestion of a heel imprint and a rounded toe. She guessed that the person had been wearing boots, but she wasn't sure.

After a moment, Samantha sighed. "I wish we'd seen these footprints earlier, before the wind started to blow. The only thing I can tell now is that the person came from that way." She pointed toward the hill, where the castle sat grimly on the rocks. "And the tracks stop here, at the library window."

Samantha and Nellie looked at each other. "Do you think it could have been Lady Florence who made these prints?" Nellie asked. "You said she was taking pictures in the castle last night."

"Maybe," Samantha said thoughtfully. "She's small, and the footprints don't look very big. But why would Lady Florence have come inside through the window? She could have used the front door." Samantha caught her breath. "*Unless* she was doing something sneaky, like taking rare books..."

Nellie looked troubled. "But she's Sir Charles's goddaughter! I don't think she would steal from him."

"Let's follow the footprints up the hill," Samantha said. "Maybe we'll find more clues near the castle."

Nellie thought for a moment. "All right," she said finally. "I want to help Ian and Henry if we can. But I hope Sir Reginald's ghost isn't up there today."

The cold wind tossed the girls' hair and chilled their noses as they climbed to the top of the hill. A few times they saw tracks that might have been boot prints. But as the path grew rockier, the tracks grew fainter. The last part of the path was the steepest, and Nellie and Samantha were breathless when they reached the top. They both searched the wind-swept hilltop. The footprints seemed to have disappeared.

Even in the sunlight, the stone ruins looked mysterious. Samantha couldn't help thinking about Sir Reginald. *It's daytime, so we should be safe from the ghost,* she told herself. Yet she and Nellie stayed close together as they walked through the archway and into the castle.

The thick walls sheltered the ruins, and the snow here had not yet been swept away. After a few moments, Nellie stopped short. "What's this?" she asked, pointing at the ground.

Together, the girls crouched down and studied what looked like a faint footprint near the entrance to the first tower they had climbed. "Do you think it's one of our footprints from yesterday?" Nellie asked doubtfully.

"Let's check," said Samantha. The girls made their own footprints next to the mark in the snow. The girls' boots were almost identical— both had squared toes and narrow heels. They looked quite different from the rounded track in the snow.

"At least we know that it's not ours," said Samantha.

Nellie nodded. "I guess we'd better look up in the tower," she said reluctantly.

Samantha felt her heart pounding as she and Nellie entered the dark tower together. It had the damp, mossy smell that she remembered, and the ceiling was so low that she had to bend over to avoid hitting her head.

She was inching her way up the first few steps when a voice demanded, "Where are you going?"

Samantha stood up so fast that she cracked her head against the stone. "Ow!" she cried.

Then she turned around. Two freckled faces were looking up at the girls from the tower entrance. It was Ian and Henry. "Old Fish sent us to fetch you for lunch," Ian explained.

"How did you know we were here?" Nellie demanded.

"We saw you from the schoolroom window,

of course," said Henry. "You took a long time getting here, didn't you?"

"Why were you poking around the ground? Looking for arrowheads?" asked Ian.

"No!" declared Samantha. "We were looking for clues." She climbed the stairs quickly, not wanting the twins to guess that she'd ever been afraid.

"What kind of clues?" asked Henry as he and Ian started up the stairs behind them.

"We're trying to find out who stole the books," explained Nellie, and she told the boys about the footprints they had followed from the library window. "We thought that maybe the thief came up here."

When they all reached the top of the tower, Henry said, "You can see forever from up here." He leaned out over the parapet wall and scanned the hill beneath them. "I can't see any footprints, though."

"You'd have to be close to see them," said Samantha. "Besides, the wind has probably blown them away by now." She began to look around the perch to see if she could find other clues or signs that someone had been in the tower. She had a nagging feeling that she had seen *something* important the last time she was here, but she couldn't remember what it was.

As Samantha scanned the floor, she had a sudden idea. "May I see your shoes, please?" she asked the boys.

Ian stared at her. "Whatever for?"

"We just need to look at them," Nellie insisted. Ian shrugged, and then he and Henry each lifted one foot for inspection.

"No," Nellie and Samantha said together, and the boys dropped their boots back onto the stone floor.

"Your boots don't look a bit like the footprints we saw," Nellie added. "The toes are different."

Bright spots of red appeared on Henry's cheeks. "Of course they don't! Why would you think a daft thing like that? We already told you that we didn't steal the old books—even if Uncle thinks we did."

Samantha wasn't sure what *daft* meant, but she knew by Henry's tone that it wasn't good. "We believe you," she said. "But you *were* up here with us yesterday, so the footprints might've belonged to you. Now we know they don't. So maybe they belong to one of the suspects."

"Suspects?" Ian echoed.

Samantha and Nellie turned to each other. "I guess we should tell them," Nellie whispered.

Samantha nodded. "We made up a list of suspects this morning," she told the boys. "We included everyone we could think of who *might* have done it."

"Who's on the list?" asked Henry.

Nellie ticked off the names on her fingers as she said them aloud. "Lady Florence, Mr. Fisher, and all the servants—Mrs. Grissom, Mr. MacDougal, Roger, Daisy, the cook—I don't know her name."

"Mrs. Burgess," Ian supplied.

"Mrs. Burgess," Nellie repeated. She hesitated again and then added, "And Mabel."

Nellie looked down at her fingers. "That's eight people. Did we miss anyone?"

Henry thought for a moment. "There was Edith, the housemaid who left last week, but she couldn't read. I doubt she would've stolen the books."

"Probably not," Samantha agreed. "We might be able to take other names off the list, too. Grandmary told us that whoever planned the theft must be well educated."

"That takes *all* the servants off the list," said Ian. "None of them has been to school very much." He thought for a moment. "Roger is quite a good mechanic, though. He knows a lot about bicycles, but I don't think he knows anything about books."

Samantha remembered what Mabel had said about being first in her class until last summer. She was about to mention it when Nellie shot her a warning glance.

"As for the other suspects, well... Old Fish is the best tutor we've ever had," Henry said slowly. "And Florrie is some kind of cousin of ours. I can't imagine that either of them could be the thief."

"Well, *someone* took the books," Nellie reminded him.

"There's another thing, too," said Samantha. "Late last night, I heard strange noises outside Nellie's and my room. I looked out the door and saw a woman pulling a cart down the hall." She paused and then added, "I think it was Lady Florence."

"Did the cart have bicycle wheels?" asked Ian.

Samantha recalled the creaking wheels she had heard. "Yes! How did you know?"

"Florrie was having trouble pulling the cart she uses for her camera, so Ian and I put bicycle wheels on it for her. She says it works much better now," Henry explained. He looked out over the parapet wall, frowning. "But she said she'd pay us for the wheels, and she hasn't given us a penny yet. I guess she still doesn't have any money."

Samantha and Nellie looked at each other, surprised. "Isn't her father an earl?" Samantha asked. "Don't they have lots of money?"

"Yes, but her father refuses to give her spending money because she's staying here in England for the winter—instead of going to Egypt with the rest of the family," said Ian. He rubbed his hands together in the chilly wind. "If I were her, *I'd* go to Egypt—it's not nearly as cold there as it is here."

"Florrie used to be great fun," Henry added. "When we were younger, she'd play games and think up jokes, too. Now all she wants is to be a newspaper reporter, and she'll hardly even talk to us—unless she wants something, of course."

Samantha thought for a moment. "Lady Florence was in the library yesterday, and she seemed upset when we all came in. She might know something about the thefts."

Henry turned back to face them. "Florrie would do a lot to become a reporter, but she wouldn't steal anything."

"Maybe not, but she *was* wearing her coat and hat late at night," Samantha persisted. "And after she left, I saw flashes of light up here. At first, I thought it was Lady Florence's camera, but why would she take pictures up here at night? Could she have been signaling to someone?"

Henry arched his eyebrows. "She might've been looking for Sir Reginald's ghost," he suggested. "She's been asking Uncle about the ghost ever since she got here."

"We came up here at dusk once looking for the ghost, too," added Ian, looking down on the ruins. "But all we ever found was an arrowhead."

"Of course! The arrowhead!" exclaimed Samantha. She finally knew what had been nagging at her. She searched in her pocket and pulled out the gray button she had found. "Look at this," she said, holding the button up to the sunlight. "I saw the edge of it sticking up in the snow yesterday. I thought it might be an arrowhead at first."

Ian scowled. "It doesn't look a bit like an arrowhead."

"I know that now," said Samantha impatiently.

"But it *was* left up here recently—there wasn't even much snow on it. And the tracks from the library lead up here, so it could be a clue. Does it look familiar?"

Both Henry and Ian shook their heads, but Nellie, who had often had to mend clothes when she worked as a maid, examined the button closely. "Well," she said at last, "there's nothing fancy about it. I'd guess that it came from some plain, everyday sort of clothes. I wonder who lost it."

"Maybe we should look for whoever's missing a button and then tell Uncle who the thief is," Ian said hopefully.

"We'd have to be sure before we said anything," Nellie cautioned. "We wouldn't want to send the wrong person to jail."

"Yes," Samantha agreed. "We'd need proof."

Henry shrugged. "Anyone might've lost an old button. I don't see how it helps us." He turned back to look out over the parapet again. After a moment, he whistled softly. "That's interesting..."

"What?" the others demanded, craning their necks to see.

"See that carriage in front of the house?" he said, pointing down the hill. "The driver is loading boxes on it, and Florrie is out there, too. It looks like she's giving him directions." Henry turned to face the others. "I wonder if she's going away. If she is, why didn't she tell anyone?"

Samantha remembered the quiet footsteps from the night before, and the plain dark clothes that Lady Florence wore. *And why did she sneak out of the house in the middle of the night?* she wondered.

"We have to talk with Lady Florence before she leaves!" Samantha declared, and she turned around and began running down the twisty steps of the tower.

7

A CHASE

Samantha, Nellie, Ian, and Henry hurried down the rocky path toward the manor house. When they arrived at the front door, they found the driver still loading boxes into the carriage. Lady Florence was nowhere in sight.

"Why is that carriage here, Roger?" Henry asked as the footman took their coats and hats.

"Lady Florence requested it, Master Henry," said Roger in a formal voice. Then he leaned forward and whispered confidentially, "Lady Florence announced that she is leaving, and she's been running around packing up everything. Quite a flurry she's in!"

"Where is Lady Florence now?" Samantha asked.

Before the footman could answer, the jangle

of Mrs. Grissom's keys echoed down the hall.

"Hide!" whispered Henry. "We can't let her send us upstairs!"

Henry ducked into the small coatroom, and Samantha, Nellie, and Ian followed close behind. Only a thin ribbon of light came into the room from under the door. Pressed between wool coats that smelled of mothballs, Samantha listened as Mrs. Grissom called to the footman, "Roger, I thought I heard the children!"

"Yes, ma'am, they're back," Roger replied.

"Did they go up to the schoolroom?" demanded Mrs. Grissom.

Roger had watched the children slip into their hiding place. He hesitated, and then he said loudly enough for them to overhear, "The children left here just a short time ago, ma'am."

"Too bad they're not gone for good!" Mrs. Grissom declared. She heaved a sigh. "I hear Sir Charles is sending the boys back to school next week. I can hardly wait!"

"Yes, ma'am," Roger murmured.

The jingling of the keys faded away as

Mrs. Grissom continued down the hall. "I told you Gruesome hates us!" Ian whispered to the others.

He had just started to open the door when footsteps clicked down the hall again. They heard Roger say, "May I help you, Lady Florence?" Samantha peeked out the door and saw Lady Florence dressed in a neat, dark gray traveling suit and a matching hat.

"Yes, Roger," Lady Florence said briskly. "Please ask the driver to load this box onto the carriage. And tell him I'll be ready shortly."

Henry opened the closet door wide, and all four children tumbled out. Lady Florence stepped back in surprise. "Are you going away, Florrie?" Henry asked her innocently.

Lady Florence scrunched up her face. "I told you not to call me Florrie anymore!" she reminded Henry. "I'm too old for that now." Then she took a deep breath and pushed a stray strand of her hair back into its bun. "And yes, I'm taking the 2:45 train to London. I'm sorry I have to leave without saying good-bye to

Uncle, but something rather important has come up." Lady Florence turned to walk away.

Samantha, desperate to stop her, blurted out, "Excuse me, is this your button?" She held up the dark gray button that happened to be just the same color as Lady Florence's suit.

"It was in the castle tower," Nellie added.

"I'm not aware of having lost a button," said Lady Florence without much interest. "You girls may certainly keep it if you wish."

"But you *have* been in the castle tower," Henry persisted. "Were you by any chance there last night?"

Lady Florence snapped around to face him. "Why do you ask?"

"There were flashes of light up there in the middle of the night," Ian told her.

"And we wondered if you might be taking photographs in the dark," Henry said.

Lady Florence bit her lip. "Please don't tell Uncle!" she whispered to the boys. "Not yet! He'll find out soon anyhow and—" Just then there was a jangling sound, and Mrs. Grissom

strode back into the entry hall. Lady Florence
drew herself up as tall as she could and, in her
normal voice, added, "Now, if you'll excuse me,
I have a lot to do." Then she turned and walked
away quickly.

Samantha wanted to race after Lady Florence.
But Mrs. Grissom had stopped in the middle
of the entry hall, her hands on her hips. "I've
been looking all over for you!" the housekeeper
told the twins. "Your luncheon is waiting in
the schoolroom."

"We'll be there in a minute, Mrs. Grissom,"
said Henry distractedly as Lady Florence disappeared around the corner.

"We need to go talk to our cousin," Ian
added.

"Master Henry and Master Ian, you are
already quite late!" Mrs. Grissom said decidedly.
"You must all go upstairs now. I will escort you
myself."

Despite the boys' protests, the housekeeper
accompanied them all the way up the stairs
and into the schoolroom. "Ah, there you are at

last," said the tutor as he put away the book he'd been reading.

Samantha was surprised to see both Daisy and Mabel waiting for them, too. The maids were dressed in clean white aprons and caps, and they were standing patiently by the food. Suddenly Samantha realized that luncheon at Lockston Manor was not just a meal, it was a formal event.

Lady Florence will be gone by the time we finish! she realized, and she sank down into her chair with a heavy heart.

For the first course, Daisy set out a tureen of creamy vegetable soup served with fresh rolls. Samantha, Nellie, Henry, and Ian all finished the soup course as quickly as possible. While their second course, roast beef with gravy and potatoes, was being served, Henry jumped up and looked out the window.

"Henry, what are you doing?" the tutor asked sharply. "You have not been excused from the table."

"There was a carriage at the door. I wanted to see if it was still there," said Henry as he dropped back into his chair. He gave the girls a significant look. "It's driving away now."

"Yes," said the tutor, wiping his mouth with his napkin. "I heard that Lady Florence is leaving. It's rather sudden, I'm afraid. She wasn't even able to stay long enough to say good-bye to her godfather, Sir Charles."

We've missed her! Samantha thought desperately. *Now we may never find out the truth.*

"May we go into the village after we finish eating?" Henry asked the tutor. His voice sounded deceptively casual. "The girls said they wanted to go."

Samantha and Nellie exchanged a glance. They hadn't said anything of the sort. But this time Samantha didn't mind Henry speaking for her. The tutor seemed to consider the request.

"Very well," he said at last. "You may finish your lessons later. It would be nice for our guests to see the village. It has quite an interesting history, actually . . ."

For the rest of the meal, the tutor talked about what the village had been like centuries before, when England had been at war with France, and knights like Sir Reginald had defended their country. Samantha could hardly pay attention to the tutor's lecture. She was trying to eat her meat and potatoes as fast as she could. But as Mabel cleared away the plates, Samantha noticed that the young housemaid was listening closely to Mr. Fisher.

It's too bad Mabel can't go to school anymore, Samantha thought. *It seems as if she really wants to learn more.*

As Mabel carried the heavy tray of dishes out of the room, Daisy served a flaky, cinnamon-scented apple tart for dessert. It was delicious, but none of the children had taken more than a few bites before Henry said, "May we be excused, sir? We'd like to get going if we could."

"Are you finished already?" asked the tutor as he took another bite of his tart.

"Yes!" Samantha and Nellie answered.

Ian looked yearningly at his unfinished apple tart. "Yes, I suppose," he answered with considerably less enthusiasm.

A Chase

"Very well." The tutor dismissed them with a wave. "Be sure you're back for teatime."

All four children jumped up from their chairs and rushed out the door. "If Florrie is on the 2:45 train, we'll have to hurry to get to the station before she leaves," said Henry as they galloped down the stairs.

The main hall was deserted. Henry led the way into the coatroom, and they all grabbed their hats and coats. "How long will it take us to walk to the village?" Nellie asked.

"Too long," said Henry, running out the huge main door. "That's why we're going to ride. Let's go to the stable."

"Good idea," said Ian, who was close behind his brother.

The stable! Samantha thought with alarm. "I'm not very good at riding a horse," she told the boys.

"I'm not, either," Nellie admitted.

"Doesn't matter!" replied Henry.

Puzzled, Samantha and Nellie hurried after the boys to a long, low building behind the manor house. The stable smelled of old hay and manure, but there were no horses inside, just an ancient carriage and two tandem bicycles. "These belonged to our mum and dad," said Ian, heading toward the bicycles. "When they were alive, we all rode together."

Henry pointed to the closest bicycle. "You girls take that one. Come on!"

Samantha had never ridden a tandem before, but soon she and Nellie were pedaling along the winding road to the village, past farmhouses, fields, the old broken bridge, and the stone church. Samantha, who had more experience riding bicycles, was in charge of steering. It was harder than she had expected, and she struggled to keep the tandem on the road as the wind whipped across her face.

We've got to get there in time, she thought as she and Nellie pedaled hard.

Finally, they reached the railway station. They leaned the bicycles against the building and ran inside. "Has my cousin, Lady Florence Frothingham, been here?" Henry asked the man behind the ticket counter.

The lines in the man's skin deepened as he considered this question for a moment. "A pretty young lady, with lots of boxes and trunks?"

"Yes," Samantha said. "She hasn't left yet, has she?"

The man nodded toward a pile of trunks in the corner. "She bought her ticket, and then she said she wanted to get some books before the train left. She's probably at Henderson's, across the street."

The children rushed over to a small shop with a hanging sign that read *Henderson's Books*. As they entered the musty-smelling shop, they saw Lady Florence immediately. She was carrying a folded newspaper under one arm, and there was a book on the counter in front of her. Samantha's eyebrows shot up when she saw the hand-lettered notice on the counter. It read:

Old and Rare Books
Bought and Sold

Lady Florence could have sold the rare books here! Samantha realized.

When Lady Florence turned and saw the children, her eyes widened. "Oh, it's you again," she exclaimed. Then she sighed. "Did Uncle Charles find out?"

They stared at her. "It *was* you?" Samantha burst out.

Lady Florence looked annoyed. "Of course it's me! My name's on it, isn't it?" She tilted her chin up. "And I'm proud of it."

Ian looked shocked. "You're *proud* of stealing Uncle's books?"

"Stealing? What are you talking about, you daft boy? I didn't steal anything," Lady Florence declared. She took out the newspaper, opened it to page seven, and pointed to an article. "This is what I'm proud of!"

Samantha gasped as she read the headline:

Does Ancient Ghost Haunt Lockston Castle?
by Florence R. Frothingham

Below the headline, there were two pictures of the ruined castle. The ruins looked even more abandoned and frightening in the photographs than they did in real life. Samantha scanned the article quickly. The reporter, Lady Florence, described the legend of Sir Reginald's ghost, and she gave a first-person account of seeing an eerie white figure standing in the castle tower, outlined against the night sky.

"Jiminy!" Samantha exclaimed. She looked up at Lady Florence. "Is that why you were outside last night? You really were taking photographs of the castle?"

"I tried to," Lady Florence admitted. "I knew it was too late for this story," she added, gesturing to the newspaper. "But I hope to write more articles about the ghost in the future." Lady Florence sighed. "When you asked me earlier if I'd been to the castle, I thought you'd seen today's article—and you were going to tell Uncle Charles all about it."

"Why did you want to keep the article a secret?" asked Nellie.

"Uncle Charles says that women have no business writing for newspapers," Lady Florence said. She pushed a long lock of red hair back under her hat. "I don't think he'll be very happy when he sees that I've written an article about Lockston."

"You're right," Henry agreed solemnly.

"But guess what!" said Lady Florence, brightening. "The newspaper's editor liked my article *very* much. So I asked him if I could write about the mummies in Egypt, too. He thought it was a wonderful idea! In fact, he wants me to write a series of articles about what archaeologists are discovering in the pyramids."

"So you're going to Egypt after all?" Ian asked. He sounded confused.

"Yes!" Lady Florence replied. She picked up the book on the counter, and Samantha could now see its title clearly. It was *A Visitor's Guide to Egypt*. "My parents will be happy—and I'll have a chance to write lots more articles, too." She smiled triumphantly. "My career is finally beginning!"

How exciting! thought Samantha.

A rumbling sound came from the distance. "The train is arriving," said Lady Florence, gathering up her things. "I telegraphed my parents and told them to expect me. And I'll write to Uncle Charles as soon as I'm on the ship to Egypt!"

"Wait," called Samantha as Lady Florence headed for the door. "What about the books that were stolen? Do you know anything about them?"

Lady Florence paused. "No, that was a complete surprise, actually," she admitted. "Maybe the thief is someone who loves old books. But I did see something strange."

"What?" all the children asked at once.

"It was the night I saw the ghost in the castle tower," Lady Florence recalled. "I was watching from my window. There was fog on the ground, but not long after the ghost vanished, I could have sworn I saw a white figure cross the lawn and then disappear right through the library window."

"*Through* the window?" Samantha echoed.

"It looked that way," said Lady Florence. "I ran downstairs, but when I got to the library, it was empty." She shrugged. "Maybe the library is haunted, too."

Outside, the train whistle screeched. "Now I must go," Lady Florence declared. "Good-bye!" she called, and the door slammed behind her.

8

THE FIGURE IN WHITE

When Samantha, Nellie, and the twins arrived back at the manor house, their cheeks were red from the cold and their boots smelled faintly of manure from the stable, where they had hurriedly stashed the bicycles on their return. But Mr. Fisher didn't seem to notice anything unusual as they filed into the schoolroom for tea.

"Did you have a pleasant time?" he asked, glancing up from the book he had been reading.

The children looked at each other. "It was interesting," said Henry finally.

"Ah, yes, there is so much to be learned in the village," said the tutor, closing his book. "I only wish that I had more time to study the history here."

"Where will you go, sir, when we go back to

Bristwell?" asked Ian. He looked suspiciously at the cream pitcher before pouring a generous amount into his tea.

"Oh, I'll find somewhere else to teach," said Mr. Fisher. "But I will be sorry to leave my research on this area unfinished."

"Have you learned any more about Sir Reginald?" Nellie asked the tutor.

"Why, yes," said Mr. Fisher. He beamed with pleasure. "I've found several references to Sir Reginald in old documents. He seems to have been a favorite of the king's, and he was a scholar as well as a brave soldier. He loved his family, too—perhaps that's why he risked so much to come back to them."

Maybe Sir Reginald is **still** *trying to come back to his family,* thought Samantha with a shiver. She saw that Nellie and Henry looked worried, too, and Ian hadn't even tasted his buttered scone.

Samantha remembered what Lady Florence had told them about the ghostly figure near the library. She turned to the tutor. "Would there be any reason for Sir Reginald's ghost to haunt the library?" she asked.

She half-expected the tutor to chuckle at the question, but he looked serious as he considered his answer. "Well, I've never believed in ghosts," he said finally. "But, of course, there is a connection between Sir Reginald and that part of the house."

"There is?" Henry asked.

"Oh, yes," said the tutor. "As you know, the library is in the corner of the manor house closest to the castle. Before the house was built, there was an enormous oak tree in that spot—and according to legend, that's where Sir Reginald died."

There was silence in the schoolroom after the tutor made his pronouncement. Finally, Ian spoke up. "Nobody ever told us that before," he said. He broke off a corner of the scone and looked at it mournfully.

"Well, I daresay your uncle and I have uncovered some history that's not well known," said the tutor, taking another sip of his tea.

"Yes, I'm very sorry I won't be able to continue my research."

Research! thought Samantha. With a chill, she remembered how the tutor had gone to the library yesterday for his research. She glanced at the stack of leather-bound books on the table. *Grandmary said the thief must be well educated,* she thought. *And Lady Florence thought it was someone who loved old books.*

Samantha looked at the tutor calmly drinking his tea. Was it possible that this scholarly man was actually a thief? Samantha hated to think it might be true, but Mr. Fisher now seemed the most likely suspect in the house. She reached into her pocket and pulled out the button. "Excuse me, sir, did you by any chance lose this?"

Mr. Fisher looked surprised by her question. He squinted at the button. "Not that I recall," he said. Then he smiled at Samantha. "Even if I had, I probably wouldn't have noticed. Is it important?"

"I, um, found it in one of the castle towers," said Samantha as she pocketed the button.

"Ah, the castle towers!" exclaimed Mr. Fisher. He leaned back in his chair and began to tell the children about how the towers had been cleverly constructed to ward off invaders—and how there might even have been secret passages at one time.

Mr. Fisher's lecture was interesting. But Samantha kept worrying that the tutor might be hiding a secret of his own. *We have to find out the truth,* she thought. *But how?*

After tea, Mr. Fisher directed the boys to work on their school lessons. As Samantha and Nellie went downstairs, Nellie whispered, "You seem upset. Is something wrong?"

"Let's talk in our room," Samantha whispered back.

When the girls reached their room, however, they found Mabel inside. She looked as if she had been sitting on Samantha's bed, but she jumped up when she saw them and began flicking a feather duster over the nightstand.

"Hello," said Samantha.

"Good afternoon, Miss Samantha, Miss Nellie," said Mabel, avoiding their eyes. She stepped toward the door. "I was just tidying."

"You don't have to leave," Nellie said. But Mabel was already hurrying out of the room.

As soon as Mabel had closed the door behind her, Samantha sat down on her bed. She was surprised to see her Sherlock Holmes book lying open on the pillow.

"That's funny," Samantha said. She ran her fingers over the pages. "I know I didn't leave the book open today. And this isn't the page where I stopped reading, either." She looked at Nellie. "Do you think Mabel was reading it? She looked awfully nervous when she saw us."

"Maybe," said Nellie. Her face was very serious. "But we have to be sure not to let Mrs. Grissom know. Mabel could be fired for such a thing."

"Fired? Just for reading?"

Nellie nodded. "Once when I was working for

Mrs. Ryland, I stopped for just a moment to look at a picture in a newspaper. Mrs. Ryland saw me and said she didn't pay me to be lazy. She made me spend the rest of the day cleaning the cellar."

"That's terrible!" said Samantha sadly. "Mabel doesn't have any friends here, and she's not allowed to read books, either." Samantha remembered the eager look on Mabel's face as she had listened to Mr. Fisher's lecture. "It must be awfully lonely."

Samantha closed the Sherlock Holmes book and put it on top of the nightstand. Then she sat on her bed and stared at the book for a moment. She felt her stomach twist with anxiety.

"Nellie," she said at last, "remember how Grandmary said that the thief had to be educated—and Lady Florence thought it might be someone who likes books?"

"Yes," said Nellie. "Why?"

"Well, I just realized that description could fit Mr. Fisher—*or* Mabel." Samantha pulled the button from her pocket and handed it to Nellie. "You said that this looks like a plain, everyday sort of button. Couldn't it be from the sort of clothes that a maid wears?"

Nellie sat down on her bed across from Samantha and examined the button under the bedside lamp. "It could be," she admitted. "That doesn't mean that Mabel's the thief, though. Besides, Mabel's our age. How could she have stolen the books and then replaced them? I'll bet she hardly ever gets to leave the house at all."

"It could be that Mabel was only helping someone else," Samantha suggested. "Mabel might've taken the valuable books and left them in the castle tower for someone else to pick up— and then that person could have given her the new books to put in the cabinet."

"Maybe," Nellie said reluctantly. "But we don't have any proof. Besides, if whoever took the books was only helping someone else, then any of the servants could have done it. If you were just the helper, you wouldn't have to be well educated at all. You'd just have to be able to read the titles."

"You're right!" said Samantha with relief,

and she sat back on her bed. She liked both Mabel *and* Mr. Fisher, and she didn't want to believe that either of them was the thief. But then she realized with dismay that their list of suspects now included all the servants.

"It *could've* been anyone—Mr. MacDougal, Mrs. Grissom, Daisy, Lily, Roger—anyone!" Samantha said slowly. She reached for her pillow and hugged it. For a moment, she just wanted to give up. Then she thought again of Henry and Ian being forced to go back to Bristwell. She looked up at Nellie. "We *have* to find out who the thief really is. And I have an idea."

"What?" asked Nellie, sitting up straighter.

"Well, this is our last night here, and we know that *something* strange is happening in the library. Why don't we keep watch there tonight? We can hide and see if the thief comes back."

Nellie's eyes widened. "What if someone comes in . . . but it's not the thief? What if it's the ghost?"

Samantha scrunched her pillow in her arms. "I guess we'd run away."

"And scream," added Nellie with a shudder.

"We should scream as loud as we can. Maybe that would scare the ghost away."

When Henry and Ian heard about the girls' plan, they insisted on joining in. "Old Fish always goes to bed at nine o'clock," Henry whispered after supper. "As soon as he goes to his room, we'll come knock at your door, and then we'll all go down to the library together."

"All right," Samantha agreed. "But no tricks this time!"

"We promise," Henry said solemnly.

"The last thing we want is to go back to Bristwell," added Ian. "We want to catch the thief even more than you do!"

But that evening, the girls waited and waited in their room. At half past nine, there was still no sign of the twins. Samantha and Nellie had almost decided to go by themselves when there was a soft knock at the door.

"Sorry we're late," said Henry. "This was the

one night when Old Fish stayed up working."

"Let's hurry," said Samantha. The four children walked as quietly as they could along the corridor and down the winding staircase to the main hall. With Sir Charles, Grandmary, and the Admiral out for the evening and Lady Florence gone for good, the huge house seemed deserted. The only sound they heard was Roger's voice in a distant hallway.

Samantha opened the door to the library, and they all tiptoed in. It was so dark inside that Ian stumbled over a chair. "Let's turn on a light," he whispered.

"No! We don't want the thief to know that anyone's here," Henry whispered back.

"But we'll turn on the light if anyone comes," Samantha added.

Henry and Ian stood in the shadows near the rare-book cabinet, while Samantha and Nellie hid by Lady Stallsworth's desk. Samantha felt her heart pounding as she and Nellie crouched close together in the darkness. In the distance, she heard Roger say something. Daisy laughed, and then Mr. MacDougal spoke sharply. *Could the thief be one of them?* Samantha wondered. She breathed a little easier when their voices faded away.

In the silence that followed, she listened to every creak of the old house. She sat straight up when she heard a faint rustling noise somewhere in the library.

"I think it's a mouse," Nellie whispered.

Samantha relaxed slightly. But she kept listening. The only sounds were the faint whistle of the wind outside and the boys' occasional whispers. *Maybe this was a silly idea*, she thought finally. *Maybe no one is coming at all.*

Then she heard the soft crunch of footsteps in the snow outside. The sound grew closer. Suddenly, there was a loud creak, and a cold rush of air swept into the room. Samantha heard a thump. She could hardly breathe as she looked toward the window.

The curtains moved, and Samantha froze in fear as a white figure appeared.

9
SEARCH FOR A SECRET

As the pale figure moved closer, Samantha knew she had to act. She forced herself to reach for the lamp. For a moment, she fumbled in the darkness, trying to find the switch. Then the light clicked on. Samantha stared at the figure in the middle of the library.

It wasn't a ghost at all. It was a person covered head to toe by a pale gray cloak. The cloak was dusted with snow and shone almost white in the dim light.

The cloaked figure gasped and then tried to rush for the door. But Samantha had already recognized the curly, light brown hair under the hood.

"Mabel?" she exclaimed in disbelief.

The housemaid turned around to face her.

Samantha could see now that Mabel was carrying an unlit candle in her hand. She looked as shocked as Samantha felt.

The boys hurried from the other side of the library. "It's the housemaid!" said Ian.

"She must be the thief," declared Henry.

Mabel tossed back the hood of her cloak and glared at him. "I'm not a thief!" she said defiantly. "My work for the day is finished. I only went outside for a little while."

"You expect us to believe that?" Henry demanded.

"Only thieves go sneaking around at night," said Ian with an air of victory. He started for the door. "Keep an eye on her, Henry. I'll tell Mr. MacDougal."

Mabel's face turned as white as her cloak. "No!" she pleaded. "Please. I promise you, I haven't done anything wrong!"

But Ian was already at the door.

"Wait!" Nellie called to him. Her blue eyes looked troubled. "Don't tell Mr. MacDougal yet. Let's listen to what Mabel has to say. We don't want to get her into trouble if she hasn't done anything wrong."

Ian stopped. "But we practically caught her red-handed!" he protested.

"Nellie's right," insisted Samantha, who still hoped that Mabel might have an explanation. "We should listen first." She turned and put a hand on Mabel's arm. "Why did you go outside by yourself at night?" she asked kindly. "Isn't that scary?"

Samantha's gentle question seemed to take Mabel by surprise. "I miss my mother and my sisters," said Mabel, and tears started to roll down her cheeks. "And I can't get home!"

"Oh, for goodness' sake," Henry sighed. "Now she's turning on the waterworks!" But both he and Ian lent Mabel their handkerchiefs. Then the boys stood back as Samantha and Nellie led Mabel to an armchair in the corner of the library.

Mabel sat down and dried her eyes. "I'm the oldest of three girls in my family," she began.

"I am, too," said Nellie softly.

Mabel went on to explain that her family owned a small farm, and they had once had a comfortable life. "My mum was a teacher before she married Dad, and I hoped to be a teacher too someday," she said with pride in her voice.

But, Mabel said, her father had died two years ago. Since then, the farm had suffered and the family had gone into debt. To help her mother, Mabel had taken a job at the manor house as soon as she turned twelve years old.

"The farm is just on the other side of the river, and I thought I'd be able to see my mother and sisters every week," she continued. "But after I started work, there was a storm, and the bridge broke apart. Now I have to walk eight miles to get home, and Mrs. Grissom hardly ever gives me enough time off. It's been months since I've seen my family. My mother's been sick, too, and I worry about her all the time."

"But what does all that have to do with going outside at night?" asked Henry. "You can't swim across the river, can you?"

"Of course not," said Mabel. "But last summer,

my sister Martha and I found that we could signal each other. On clear nights, I climb up the castle tower and light a candle. Martha watches for me with our father's old spyglass, and she lights three candles in the top window of our house." Mabel took a deep breath. "If I see the candles, I know everyone at home is safe."

For a moment, no one spoke. Samantha felt ashamed. She had suspected Mabel of stealing, but Mabel, who was so alone here at the manor, had only wanted a signal from home. Samantha pulled the button out of her pocket and showed it to Mabel. "Is this yours?"

"Oh, yes!" Mabel took the button eagerly. "I was looking for it. Where did you find it?"

"In the castle tower," said Samantha.

A strange look passed over Ian's face. "Are *you* the ghost that everyone has been seeing?"

Suddenly, Mabel looked embarrassed. "Well, no, I mean yes—well, I didn't mean to be at first," she stammered. "Then people started talking about seeing the ghost in the castle tower. I knew it was probably me they'd seen, but I couldn't say anything, could I? I'd have lost my job." Mabel hesitated. "Then, later, yes—I began to wear this cloak, so that if people did see anything, they'd think it was the ghost, not me."

Henry folded his arms across his chest. "But why did you steal Uncle Charles's books?"

"I told you, I didn't steal anything!" Mabel said. "I didn't even *borrow* any books from the library, I swear!"

"You must have *some* reason for coming into the library," insisted Henry.

Mabel pointed to the window where she'd entered. "Once when I was dusting, I saw that the window over there doesn't close quite right. If you jiggle it, you can open it from the outside, even if it looks like it's locked. This part of the house is closest to the castle, so I could get out without people seeing me—well, except Lady Stallsworth, that is. She saw me once."

"Lady Stallsworth knew what you were doing?" Nellie asked her.

"Not at first," said Mabel. "But one night

when I came back to the library, a light was on. I couldn't hear anyone, though, so I took a chance and opened the window. I was halfway inside when I saw Lady Stallsworth. She was standing by the glass cabinet with all the fancy books in it. She looked upset, as if she'd been crying. I was afraid she was going to be angry with me, but she told me to sit down and we talked. Her ladyship was very kind. She even said that she'd tell Mrs. Grissom that I should have more time to see my family."

"That sounds like Aunt Emily," Ian confirmed. "She was always nice to everyone."

Mabel nodded, and her eyes filled with tears. "Her ladyship asked me if I liked to read," Mabel recalled. "I told her I did, and she said I could borrow books whenever I felt lonely. Then she told me that she had to finish a very important letter, but she wasn't feeling well and she was too tired to write any more. She said I should go upstairs to bed, and she'd talk to me in the morning. But..." Mabel paused and shook her head.

"What happened?" asked Henry.

"We never had a chance to talk. The next morning, Lady Stallsworth fainted during morning prayers. She died that night."

For a moment the library was silent. Samantha looked up at Lady Stallsworth's portrait above the fireplace, and she felt a shiver go down her back. It was almost as if Lady Stallsworth was looking right at her.

From somewhere not too far away came the rumbling of Roger's voice, followed by Daisy's tinkling laughter. Mabel snatched off her snowy cloak and folded it into a tight bundle. "I have to go," she said nervously. "I can't let anyone else find me here."

Henry and Ian exchanged a glance, and then both boys nodded. Henry looked out the door. "The coast is clear," he reported, and Mabel escaped down the hall.

Left alone in the library, the four children gathered around the circle of light given off by the desk lamp. "What do we do now?" asked Ian. "If Mabel's telling the truth—"

"I'm sure she is!" Nellie said.

"I believe her, too," Samantha agreed.

Henry sighed. "Well then, who did take the books? If we don't find the thief, we might as well pack our trunks for Bristwell."

Samantha thought back to the list of suspects that she and Nellie had written. "If it wasn't Lady Florence or Mabel," she said slowly, "that leaves only the other servants and Mr. Fisher."

"We told you that it couldn't be Old Fish," said Henry, tapping on the desk with a pencil. "He's always going on about 'doing the honorable thing' and all that."

"Yes," Ian agreed. "He doesn't know much about bicycles, but besides that, he's absolutely top-notch. I can't imagine him stealing sixpence, much less a rare book."

"All the servants have been here a long time, too," said Henry. "Everyone except Mabel, that is." He shook his head. "I'm still not sure we should believe her."

Suddenly, Samantha had an idea. "Mabel said that Lady Stallsworth had been standing near the rare books, and she seemed upset about something," Samantha recalled. "What if Lady Stallsworth knew what had happened to her books, and she was going to tell somebody about it?"

"The only problem is, she never *did* tell anyone," Henry pointed out. "At least as far as we know. So what good does it do?"

"But Lady Stallsworth might have left a clue in the letter she was writing," Samantha suggested. "If only we could find it."

Henry looked down at Lady Stallsworth's old-fashioned desk. It was made of beautifully polished wood. At the back of the writing surface, there was a small, delicately carved compartment that held a shelf for pens. On either side of the carved compartment were several drawers and cubbyholes for storing letters and supplies. Below the desktop were four large drawers, each with a decorated brass handle.

The desktop was empty now, except for a leather desk blotter covered with a paper pad for catching ink stains. "There's no letter here now," said Henry, surveying the desk. He shrugged. "Maybe Aunt Emily sent it off in the post."

"I don't think that's likely," said Nellie with growing confidence. "Mabel said Lady Stallsworth was too tired to finish the letter that night, and I doubt she would have had time to finish it in the morning, either. It might still be in the desk somewhere."

Together, the children searched the desk. First they opened the big drawers, but all they found were account books from the manor, carefully dated and arranged. Next, they looked into the cubbyholes and drawers on top of the desk. They found a silver pen and a matching inkwell, several pencils, a letter opener, a magnifying glass, stamps, an address book, and blank sheets of paper and envelopes. But there was no sign of an unfinished letter.

Staring at the desk, Samantha remembered a Sherlock Holmes detective story she'd read. She picked up the leather desk mat and held the blotting pad close to the light. There was a single large ink stain on the pad and several smaller stains.

"You're supposed to be able to see what a person was writing just by looking at the blotter that was under the paper," she told the others. "As the person presses down on the pen to write, it leaves marks on the blotter. Maybe we can see what Lady Stallsworth wrote."

"Really?" said Ian. He studied the blotter over Samantha's shoulder. Nellie and Henry craned their necks to get a better look, too.

"What do you see?" asked Henry after a moment.

Samantha squinted at the blotter. "I'm not sure," she said. She reached for the magnifying glass and studied the blotter more closely. Finally, she put down the glass. "All I see are little dents that look like lines and squiggles," she confessed. "Maybe it works only if people press the pen down hard when they're writing."

"Here, let me look," said Henry. Samantha passed him the magnifying glass. "I don't see anything, either," he said after a moment.

Finally, Ian examined the blotter. "I think I see a number," he reported. "It looks like an eight or maybe a six." Ian glanced up at the others. "Do you suppose it means anything?"

"I don't know," Samantha admitted. She was beginning to feel like a failure as a detective.

While the boys were studying the blotter, Nellie stood back and eyed the desk. "What would you do if you had something important, and you didn't want anyone to see it?" she asked.

Samantha thought about the list of suspects that she had tucked into her underwear drawer, and the diary she kept in a special place in her room at home. "I'd hide it," she said.

Nellie nodded. "That's what I'd do, too."

"Oh, Nellie, you're right!" Samantha exclaimed. "If the letter was really important, Lady Stallsworth probably would have hidden it somewhere."

Samantha stepped back and examined Lady Stallsworth's desk more carefully. It reminded her of the antique desk that Grandmary had in her study at home. That desk had a secret drawer where Grandmary kept important family papers, including Samantha's birth certificate. Whenever Grandmary took out the drawer, Samantha always asked to see the certificate. She loved to look at the yellowed parchment paper where her whole name, Samantha Mary Parkington, was carefully written along with the names of her parents, who had died so long ago.

"I wonder if there could be a secret drawer in this desk," said Samantha thoughtfully. The boys were staring at her strangely. "You know," she explained, "a little drawer hidden behind all the others."

"A secret drawer?" Henry said with interest. "Let's take out everything and look."

They pulled out all the small drawers and put them on the floor, along with the lamp from the top of the desk and the blotter and all the supplies. The desk looked empty and a bit forlorn.

"I'm sorry," said Samantha as she examined the last cubbyhole. "I don't see anything. I guess I was wrong."

"Maybe not!" said Nellie. She was studying the shelf inside the carved compartment. "This shelf looks narrower than the drawers we pulled out. There could be something behind this compartment."

"Let's measure it," Ian suggested. "If it's not as deep as the drawers, we'll know for sure."

"I'll get a ruler," offered Henry. He hurried out of the library. While he was gone, Samantha, Nellie, and Ian tapped the back wall of the compartment. It sounded hollow. A few minutes later, Henry returned with a metal ruler and measured the compartment. It was at least four inches less than the depth of the drawers.

"There *is* space back there!" said Henry with growing excitement.

"Maybe we can pull out the whole compartment," suggested Ian. There was a thin opening between the carved compartment and the cubbyhole next to it. Ian and Henry slid the metal ruler into the opening. Then all four children used the ruler to pry out the compartment. They were concentrating on the task when they heard voices drifting in from the hall.

"Oh no!" said Ian. "Uncle's home!"

Henry quickly turned off the desk lamp. But it was too late. The door flew open and Sir Charles switched on the overhead light.

"I thought I saw a light on in here," he said sternly. "What are you children doing? I've already told you that—"

Sir Charles broke off. Samantha saw him staring down at Lady Stallsworth's desk. The drawers were scattered on the floor, and the ruler was stuck in behind the compartment. "What the devil is going on here?" he exploded.

Grandmary and the Admiral hurried into the room. Grandmary took in the scene with a glance. "I'm sure there's some explanation," she said. Then she looked expectantly at Samantha and Nellie.

Samantha took a deep breath. "It was my idea, Sir Charles. I—"

"No, it's all our fault, sir," Henry interrupted her. He stepped forward. "You see, we were looking for the letter, and—"

"What letter?" Sir Charles barked. "What are you talking about?"

"Perhaps you'd better start at the beginning," the Admiral suggested calmly.

Together, Samantha, Nellie, and the twins described what had happened. Samantha and Nellie tried hard to keep Mabel's secret, but Sir Charles questioned the boys and soon he learned everything.

"Great heavens!" Sir Charles said when they were finished. He strode over to the curtains and examined the window latch. "I'll have that fixed in the morning. Imagine a housemaid thinking she can come and go whenever she pleases! And I'll certainly question her about the missing books—perhaps she knows more than she told you."

Sir Charles turned to Ian and Henry, his white eyebrows bent in a stern V. "Now go up to bed before I lose my patience completely. After your shenanigans tonight, I'm jolly glad that Bristwell Academy has agreed to take you back."

"But, sir, we've found a secret drawer in the desk," Ian protested.

"Ridiculous!" sputtered Sir Charles. "There's no secret drawer. You children are only making a mess of things. Now go!"

"Please, sir," said Henry, stepping forward again. "Trust us this once. We took measurements, and we can prove that there must be something behind the compartment."

Before Sir Charles could reply, Grandmary walked to the desk. "The children may be right," she said, eyeing the antique. "My desk at home is very much like this one. Let me try something."

Grandmary reached back into the cubbyholes on either side of the compartment. She seemed to search for something. Finally she said, "Here we are!" The carved compartment swung open, revealing a hidden drawer.

Sir Charles hurried over. "Why, I never knew this was here," he said, examining the drawer.

Samantha felt a flutter in her stomach as Sir Charles pulled out two sheets of paper. *Is there a clue to the theft?* she wondered. *Did Lady*

Stallsworth have any idea who the thief could be?

At first, Sir Charles just glanced at the sheets of paper in his hand. Then he sat down heavily in the chair and studied the papers closely. "I've been a fool," he said finally, half to himself. He looked over at the twins. "Henry, Ian—I would like to speak to you boys, please."

Samantha swallowed hard, and then she looked over at Henry and Ian. Their faces were so pale that their freckles stood out like chicken pox.

Grandmary cleared her throat. "Samantha, Nellie, you go upstairs to bed now," she directed them firmly. "We must be ready to leave early tomorrow."

Reluctantly, Samantha and Nellie made their way to their room in the north wing. "What do you think Sir Charles found in the drawer?" Nellie whispered as they walked through the freezing halls.

Samantha felt her stomach do a flip-flop. "I wish I knew," she whispered back.

10
THE LETTER

In the morning, Samantha woke to the sound of clattering china. When she opened her eyes, she saw Daisy bringing in the tray of hot cocoa. "Good morning, miss," the housemaid greeted her.

Samantha sat up straight in bed. "Good morning," she replied sleepily. Then she looked around the room. "Where is Mabel? She brought us hot chocolate yesterday."

"Mabel is, er, busy," said Daisy, glancing away. "Is there anything else I can get for you, miss?"

"No, thank you," said Samantha. She looked up at Daisy anxiously. "Mabel wasn't fired, was she?"

"I really couldn't say, miss," Daisy replied. "All I know is that Mrs. Grissom asked me to take Mabel's place this morning." She glanced at the clock. "Morning prayers are in fifteen minutes, so you'd best hurry."

Samantha and Nellie rushed to wash, brush their hair, and dress. As they went downstairs, Samantha felt a cold lump of fear in her stomach. *Nellie and I were trying to help the boys,* she thought. *But I wonder if we only made things worse for them—and for Mabel.*

The girls arrived in the main hall just as Sir Charles was opening the Bible for morning prayers. As Samantha glanced around the group, she was relieved to see Mabel standing at the back of the hall, behind the plump cook. But Mr. Fisher was absent. There were dark circles under Sir Charles's eyes, and Henry and Ian looked very serious in their gray suits.

What's happened? Samantha wondered anxiously.

As soon as prayers were over, Grandmary beckoned to Samantha and Nellie. "We're all having breakfast together in the dining room this morning," she said in a low voice. "Sir

Charles expressly invited you girls."

Silently, Samantha and Nellie filed into the enormous dining room with Grandmary, the Admiral, Henry, and Ian. The dining table was crowded with platters of eggs, bacon, smoked fishes, ham, sausages, and fried tomatoes. But Samantha was too worried to be hungry.

Sir Charles took his place at the head of the table, and then he coughed significantly. "I invited you children to join us this morning because I have a most important announcement. Yesterday, I told you that there would be a reward of one hundred pounds for information leading to the discovery of whoever took *Paradise Lost*." He looked around the table. "You four children have earned that reward, and I thank you. Here it is."

He handed them each an envelope. Samantha stared at hers in astonishment. *We don't even know who the thief is*, she thought. *How can Sir Charles give us a reward?*

The Admiral noticed her confusion. "I'm sure the girls were very glad to help," he told

Sir Charles. "You needn't give them a reward."

"I insist upon it," Sir Charles replied formally. Then he smiled. "You see, I learned a great deal from the letter you found."

Henry and Ian were already ripping open their envelopes. "I got twenty-five pounds!" Henry exclaimed.

"So did I!" declared Ian.

Samantha could not control her curiosity a moment longer. She looked up at Sir Charles. "Excuse me, sir, but did the papers in the drawer tell you who took the missing books?"

"Indeed they did," said Sir Charles. He pulled the papers out of his breast pocket. "Here, you may see for yourselves," he said. He handed Samantha and Nellie a receipt from Henderson's Books. It was for the sale of a first edition of *Paradise Lost*.

Nellie studied the receipt. Then she shook her head, puzzled. "I don't understand. It looks as if Lady Stallsworth sold the book herself."

"I didn't understand at first, either," said Sir Charles, putting on his glasses. "Then I saw this. I think the boys will be interested in reading it, too." He set a page of cream-colored stationery on the table. Samantha, Nellie, Ian, and Henry crowded together to read the elegant handwriting.

Dear Charles,

Since I've become ill, I've learned that our greatest treasures on earth are the people we love. I've also learned that my books are important to me not because they are rare but because of the rare knowledge inside them. I therefore plan to sell all my first editions so that I may leave a legacy for you and our beloved nephews to enjoy.

If you are reading this, it means that I have not had time to complete my plan while I'm alive. I ask that you continue it after I'm gone.

I love you, my dearest Charles, and I always will, even from beyond the grave. My hope is that you and Henry and Ian (Here an ink stain blotted out the rest.)

Ian looked up at Sir Charles. "Aunt Emily never said what she hoped for." He sounded disappointed.

Sir Charles sighed. He said slowly, "I think she hoped that you and Henry and I would truly be a family together, even without her." Sir Charles glanced around the enormous dining room. "Your Aunt Emily left me a legacy so that I could repair this house, but she always said that she wanted it to be a *home* for all of us, not just a museum."

"Does that mean that we don't have to go back to Bristwell?" Henry asked. All four children looked up at Sir Charles hopefully.

Sir Charles hesitated. "Well, I was going to discuss that with your tutor. But he's been so busy this morning— Ah, there he is now."

Mr. Fisher limped into the room. "Sir," he said, "we keep getting telegrams and telephone calls. Newspaper reporters, guidebook writers— they've all read Lady Florence's article about the ghost, and now they want to come and see the castle for themselves. What should we do?"

"We'd better get back to work on our history," Sir Charles said decidedly. "It looks very much as if we will need it sooner than we'd thought!" Then he nodded toward the boys. "As for these young men, would you be willing to continue to teach them here?"

Mr. Fisher looked from Henry to Ian. Then he said, "I'm sorry, sir. I'd like very much to continue here, but the boys will soon need a tutor who is skilled in engineering."

Ian and Henry would like that! Samantha thought happily, and she and Nellie exchanged a grin.

But Sir Charles furrowed his brow. "The Stallsworths have always been gentlemen," he reminded Mr. Fisher. "If the boys are to continue their studies at home, they'll have no need to worry about engineering. It's hardly a proper field for them to pursue."

Mr. Fisher drew himself to his full height. "If you'll forgive me for saying so, sir, the Stallsworths have been always *leaders.* I think that with the right education, young Ian and

Henry could continue that proud tradition. They could be great inventors someday."

"Really?" Sir Charles raised his eyebrows. He thought for a moment, and then he turned back to the boys. "If Mr. Fisher will remain as your tutor, I'll find someone to help him with your engineering studies—or whatever you do with those bicycles up there."

"Hurrah!" the boys cheered, and they threw their napkins into the air.

"Excuse me, sir," said Samantha above the noise. She had to ask the question that had been weighing on her mind. "What about Mabel?"

Sir Charles folded up Lady Stallsworth's letter. "Mabel is young, and I'm sure she meant no harm," he said as he tucked the letter back inside his jacket. "I spoke to her first thing this morning, and I made it quite clear that she's never to wander around the castle again. But I'll talk to Mrs. Grissom about giving her one Sunday a month to visit her family."

One Sunday a month, thought Samantha with

a pang of disappointment. *That doesn't seem like very much.*

"That would be kind of you, Sir Charles," said Grandmary approvingly. She turned to Samantha and Nellie. "Now we'd better get ready to leave, girls. We must catch the train to London this morning—and then we'll be off to Paris!"

The next hour was a blur of packing and hurried farewells. As the girls were adding the final items to their trunks, Henry and Ian stopped by their room. "Uncle's just asked us to give a tour of the castle to a guidebook writer," Ian announced proudly.

"But before we go, we want you girls to have these," said Henry. He reached into his pocket and pulled out the two arrowheads he and Ian had found. "For souvenirs, you know," he added hastily. "You can't leave without souvenirs."

"Thank you!" Nellie and Samantha said

together. "And we'll send postcards as soon as we get to Paris," Samantha promised.

"We'll write back and tell you when we finally meet Sir Reginald," Ian offered.

Nellie frowned. "Do you think you really *will* meet the ghost?"

"You'll have to write to us and find out!" Henry said with a grin, and then he and Ian ran down the hallway together.

After Samantha and Nellie finished packing, they went down to the library so that Samantha could return the book she had borrowed. The red curtains were open this morning, and light was streaming into the room. After Samantha put the book back on its shelf, she glanced up at the portrait of Lady Stallsworth. Was it her imagination, or was Lady Stallsworth looking straight at her?

As she turned to leave, Samantha felt haunted by the sense that she had left something important undone. She looked toward the open curtains and saw the castle high on the hill. Suddenly, she realized what she needed to do. She whispered her idea to Nellie.

"Oh, yes, let's!" Nellie agreed immediately.

They found the Admiral and told him their plan. Their grandfather thought for a moment, and then he nodded. "Very well," he said. "If that's what you'd like. But we must leave in a few minutes. Be quick!"

Samantha and Nellie ran all the way up to the third floor. Mabel was in the schoolroom, wiping the table with a rag. "We want to say good-bye, Mabel," Samantha said breathlessly. "And we want *you* to have the reward. You earned it—without you, we never would have discovered Lady Stallsworth's secret."

Together, Samantha and Nellie handed Mabel their envelopes.

"For me?" asked Mabel. She dropped the rag and opened the envelopes. When she saw the money inside, she turned pale. "All of this?" she whispered. She looked up at Samantha and Nellie, searching their faces as if she was afraid they might be playing a joke on her. "Are you sure?"

"Quite sure," said Samantha, smiling. "You

deserve it more than we do."

"And maybe you could go home—and go to school again," added Nellie happily.

Bright spots of pink appeared on Mabel's cheeks. "Oh," she exclaimed, "I *could* go back to school!" Mabel stared down at the envelopes in her hands as if they were magical. "This is enough for Mum to keep our farm. And I could become a teacher, too! Mum would be ever so proud of me!"

Mabel looked up at the girls and then, with the back of her hand, she wiped tears from her eyes. "I always kept hoping, but I didn't think my dream would ever come true," she said, her voice shaking. Her tears fell as she hugged both girls. "Oh, Nellie! Samantha! Thank you so much—I'll never forget you."

The Admiral and Grandmary were waiting in the horse-drawn carriage outside when Samantha and Nellie got back downstairs. As soon as the girls hopped in, the driver flicked his reins and the carriage lurched to a start.

"Well, did your plan work out?" asked the Admiral.

"Yes," said Samantha. She wiped a tear from her eye. "I think so."

"When we first arrived, your grandmother and I thought that you girls would be fine here, even though it is a foreign country for you," said the Admiral as the carriage began to roll down the drive.

Her grandfather's voice sounded serious. *Did we do something wrong?* Samantha wondered.

But when she looked up, she saw that he was smiling. "We never guessed how well you'd both do," the Admiral continued. "After all, you girls were able to solve a mystery that puzzled everyone else."

"And you've helped a lonely girl go back to her family," added Grandmary. Her blue eyes were sparkling. "We're very proud of you both."

Samantha felt a warm glow as she turned around for one more glimpse of the castle.

THE LETTER

"Oh, Nellie, look!" she said. There were Henry and Ian, waving to them from the tower lookout.

Samantha and Nellie leaned toward their windows and waved good-bye, too, until the carriage picked up speed and the castle vanished from sight.

LOOKING BACK

A PEEK INTO THE PAST

London, the world's largest city in Samantha's time

In 1907, Samantha and Nellie lived in big, bustling New York City. But as exciting as New York was, it was much smaller than London, the first stop on Samantha and Nellie's tour of Europe.

London was the most important city in the world in the early 1900s. As the capital of England, it was the heart of the vast British Empire—the many lands around the globe that Great Britain once ruled. More than six million people lived in the city—so many that coal smoke from London's homes and factories helped create the famously thick fog that Samantha and Nellie notice on their way to the British Museum.

Wealthy Americans admired European cities such as London, Paris, and Rome because they were filled with centuries of history, art, and tradition. Compared to the relatively new United States, many Americans regarded Europe as the height of culture and sophistication.

Families who could afford to travel considered

American tourists in London

a "Grand Tour" of Europe an important part of their children's education. After traveling by steamship across the Atlantic Ocean, families spent months touring Europe. They visited museums and famous buildings, studied history, enjoyed theater and opera, and maybe even learned a foreign language. A Grand Tour was an opportunity for Americans to learn about the world—and to collect memories and souvenirs that they treasured throughout their lives.

Souvenirs of England

When Samantha and Nellie arrived in England, they discovered a country where the language and many customs were familiar. Yet there were important differences between England and America, too.

In 1907, the United States was a fast-growing country headed by an energetic president, Theodore Roosevelt. People from around the world saw America as a place of opportunity. In 1907 alone, more than a million immigrants arrived in New York City. Like Nellie's parents, who had come from Ireland, most immigrants were poor, and they had to struggle when they arrived in America— often laboring in factories or as servants. But

immigrants came to America because they believed that if they worked hard, they could give their families a better future.

England, in contrast, was a very old country where people's social class was often

Immigrants believed that America offered the hope of a better future.

decided mostly by who their parents were. England's king, for example, held the throne because he was the oldest son in the royal family. In the story, Florence Frothingham is called "Lady Florence" because she is the daughter of an earl and is therefore a member of the *nobility*, or the noble class. The children of nobility inherited high social position just as they often inherited wealth and titles.

Edward VII became king of England after his mother, Queen Victoria, died in 1901.

Members of the *landed gentry*—the wealthy landowners of England—were not nobility, but they were also very proud of their family's position and history. Someone like Sir Charles, whose family had owned Lockston Manor for generations, was an important and respected person.

An imposing English manor house

English housemaids in the early 1900s

The servants who kept a grand house like Lockston Manor running were expected to "know their place" and remain as invisible as possible to the family and their guests. A maid like Mabel would have been required to work hard. She might have cleaned, polished, and run errands from morning until night, with little time to herself. But maids and other servants usually remained in the lower classes of society, no matter how hard they worked.

Important changes were coming to both England and America when Samantha was a girl, however. Exciting new inventions such as

A gramophone, or early record player, one of many inventions that became popular in Samantha's time

electric lights, telephones, automobiles, and bicycles were quickly changing everyday life in both countries.

As England became more modern, some people worried that the treasures of the past might be lost. Like Sir Charles, they began working to restore and preserve historic homes and open them to the public. Today, visitors can tour many impressive manor houses and ancient castles—and imagine what life in England was like long ago.

Many English castles are now restored and open to the public.

ABOUT THE AUTHOR

 Sarah Masters Buckey grew up in New Jersey, where her favorite hobbies were swimming in the summer, sledding in the winter, and reading all year round.

Today, she and her family live in New Hampshire. She is the author of two other mysteries featuring Samantha Parkington: *The Curse of Ravenscourt* and *The Stolen Sapphire,* as well as *The Light in the Cellar: A Molly Mystery* and *A Thief in the Theater: A Kit Mystery.*

She also wrote three American Girl History Mysteries: *The Smuggler's Treasure, Enemy in the Fort,* and *Gangsters at the Grand Atlantic.*

Many of her mysteries have been nominated for awards. Her Molly mystery, *The Light in the Cellar,* won the Agatha Award for Best Children's Mystery of 2008.

Request a FREE catalogue!

Just mail this card, call **800-845-0005**,
or visit **americangirl.com**.

Parent's name _____ / ___ / ___
Girl's birth date *(optional)*

Address _____

City _____ State _____ Zip _____

Parent's e-mail *(For order information, updates, and Web-exclusive offers.)*

(___) _____ ☐ Home ☐ Work
Phone

Parent's signature _____ 196Ii

Send a catalogue to a grandparent or friend:

Name _____

Address _____

City _____ State _____ Zip _____

Today's date ___ / ___ / ___ 152603i

Books are just the beginning...

Discover dolls, clothing, furniture,
and accessories that inspire girls
to explore their own stories.

CI07776

Welcome to
Fun for Girls!
Your million places to play!

Visit americangirl.com
and click on **Fun for Girls**
for quizzes and games.

★ **American Girl**®
PO BOX 620497
MIDDLETON WI 53562-0497

Place
Stamp
Here